EARL GREY CHRONICLES 2

A State of Affairs:
DECEPTION

Dr. AudreyAnn C. Moses

2nd Edition

OTHER BOOKS BY DR. MOSES

Dead Girl Walking...

New Renaissance: A Collection of African American Fiction

(2022)

Edited by: Dr. Rhonda Lawson

Meet The World Image Solutions

Pa-Pro-Vi Publishing 2nd Editions

Kelly Publishing 1st Editions

The Swing Novelettes

The Swing (2018) (Book 1)

Earl Grey Chronicles

Uninvited Memories (2018) (Book 1)

Saved By Grace Series

Saved by Grace: Walking Through Affliction Into God's

Deliverance (2017) (Book 1)

The Story of Wade...The Road from Darkness to

Redemption (2020) (Book 2)

Voice of Truth Publishing

RITES OF PASSAGE:

Does It Give American Black Youths the

"Right To Pass?" (2010)

(Assisted by Kenneth Nyamayaro Mufuka, Ph.D.)

Table of Contents

Acknowledgements

I just want to say Thank You Holy Spirit for clearing the fog out of my brain. To God be the Glory. Thank you to those that kept me encouraged. I would like to introduce to the world a young, brilliant artist who agreed to create my book cover, Kendra Davis. She can be found on Facebook and Instagram.

Dedication

A State of Affairs: Deception is dedicated to my family and to my shipmates of the United States Navy. Thank you for your service. It is also dedicated to everyone who feels they missed opportunities or have been mistreated at the hands of those who forgot we are all God's Children and none of us are more important, in His eyes, than the other.

"Don't judge others, and God will not judge you. 2 If you judge others, you will be judged the same way you judge them. God will treat you the same way you treat others."

(Matthew 7:1-2 ERV)

Chapter 1

*S*cotty left Natalee in 1979 to pursue his dreams of becoming a world renown lawyer. However, his road to "lawyership" was not a straight road. He expected to jump right into college and complete his education and his political plans with flying colors. He told Natalee he had the perfect opportunity to get into law school and she was not a part of that plan unless she agreed to leave the Navy and follow him.

His duty station didn't turn out to be conducive to his personal education and career plans. He was not able to finish on his timeline. Actually, it was two years before he had an opportunity to start classes on a regular basis. He neglected to include his obligations to the Army in his goals and the Army had no problems reminding him that his obligations to the Army are always the first priority of a *soldier. So, he took classes whenever he was not in the field or on assignment in some remote part of the world.*

Scotty's personal life was a shambles after he left Natalee. He wanted a relationship like his parents – financially secure and detached. He never understood love requires all of you, not part of you whenever you had nothing important to do. He always felt his looks and goals were all that should be important for any woman. He managed to have a relationship which turned into an engagement, for a short time. The same "I-know-what's-best" attitude that terminated his relationship with Natalee, terminated their engagement. He still thought his ideas were the only logical ones, and as such, he determined it was his duty to dictate his fiancé's life. She did not agree.

The only portion of his life that seemed to be under control was his military career. Unlike his father, he whole-heartedly embraced the military as a career. Scotty fell in love with the military and the military fell in love with him. He was promoted at a steady pace and was accepted into an officer program where he finally finished his bachelor's degree requirements within the top five of his class. He applied to Officer Candidate School at the United States Military Academy, WestPoint and the Naval Academy, although he did not expect to be accepted since he was Army. However, because of his grade-point average he was immediately accepted into the Naval

Academy where again he excelled. Although his beginnings was Army, he proved not only to be a quick learner, but he also adapted quickly to the "navy's way of doing things." After he completed officer candidate school he was accepted into law school where he excelled. He passed his bar exam in the top one percent of his class and was immediately offered an appointment with the Judge Advocate General Corps (JAG), his dream job. To have reached this goal was very exciting for him and, of course, his parents and grandfather were very pleased. He remembers on the day of his commissioning, and again when he completed law school, that although he was happy his family was there to congratulate him, he was sad because his biggest cheerleader, his grandmother, did not live to see this day. He often wondered if his personal life would have been less turbulent if she had lived just a little while longer.

His first five years, as a defense attorney, was in Yokosuka and Okinawa Japan. He worked with Navy, Marine and Air Force men and women, which allowed him to acquire valuable experience dealing with cases ranging from bar fights to murder to extorsion.

After his tours in Japan, he was transferred to San Diego, California for two years and then the District of Columbia. In 1996 he was assigned to Region Legal Service Office, Mid-Atlantic, Norfolk, Virginia as a prosecuting attorney. At this point Lieutenant Commander Scott was well known throughout the

Navy. His success in the courtroom, both as a defense and prosecutor, was admired.

In his assignment at the Region Legal Service Office he represents the Navy and commanding officers. He tries cases that cannot be resolved by the commanding officer. He is the Atlantic Fleet's lead prosecutor. He supervises military prosecuting lawyers, and cases, not only in Norfolk, but any military base or ship under the authority of Atlantic Fleet.

He had arrived...

Alone.

As was his habit, he shook off the perils of his love life by blaming it on the women who did not fit into his vision, even Nattie. He did not need them. For that matter, he arrived where he wanted to be with no help from any woman or anyone else. Except maybe his grandmother, and even she died too soon. When vocalizing all of his triumphs, he barely acknowledged God. Most of the time he sounded like Oscar winners as they hold their trophies in the air after reminding everyone as to why they were the only logical choice, "… oh, and by the way, thank you God for whatever it is you did. Much appreciated."

After a day of courtroom slaughtering, he laughed as he told his colleague he had no doubt about the outcome of that particular case...piece of cake. However, the smug smile on his face disappeared when he heard a text his grandmother taught him, "What profits a man to gain the whole world and lose his own soul." (Mark 8:36 KJV). She urged him to never forget where his help comes from. For a short moment he regretted the egotistic attitude he carried, at least until he felt the pats on his back from everyone in the courtroom. Then he was back to his smug self, soaking in all of that praise and adoration.

After much raising of glasses during the celebration dinner with a few friends, (if you call people you think need you more than you need them friends) he walked into a cold, uninviting apartment. There was no one there to share his victory, not even the cat. At least the cat loved him, but he had to choose between this illustrious and exclusive building and the cat. He chose the building. The cat is showing love to someone else now.

His grandfather told him if you have to make a choice make sure your final decision benefits your career and your bank account. No other choice is important.

So, here he sits...on top of the world...alone...wondering if being alone is enough and for a fleeting moment the thought flashed across his mind, "Whatever became of Nattie."

Chapter 2

September 13, 1999

"Hallucinating"

A *s he reached the top of the escalator at the MARTA station in Atlanta Georgia, a fragrance in the air drew his attention towards the open door of the train. There were at least 20 women standing on the platform and who knows how many have just stepped on the train. His eyes focused on a woman on the train sitting in a seat who immediately disappeared behind the people standing around her. Just as his brain told him to get on the train, the doors closed and the train pulled away. Even after the train was gone, he stood there, in a daze, trying to connect the dots. He was having a hard time processing what just happened and putting the pieces together. Of course the perfume is probably a favorite of many women, but he didn't know that, when he gave it to her for their first anniversary all those years ago. Who was the woman he glimpsed resembling her? How could that be? He hadn't seen her in twenty years! Why would his brain think she would be in Atlanta? She is not from Atlanta. Her people are from*

Philadelphia, or is it someplace in South Carolina, he could not remember. His imagination had to be running amuck. His brain was so clouded he almost missed the call for the train he originally intended to catch. As he stepped on the train his mind immediately remembered that awful night…the night he lost her forever.

New Year's Eve
December 31st, 1979

When he walked out of Nattie's apartment that night long ago, Scotty stood on the other side of the door already missing her and wanting to knock on the door, to beg her forgiveness for him being so selfish. He didn't. Instead he walked to his car, unlocked the door, got in the driver's seat, put the key in the ignition and just sat there. How could she not see the logic in his decision? How could she throw them away so easily, to waste her life as a clerk in the Navy? He would be a successful lawyer and would provide her with everything she ever wanted. Maybe she never loved him the way he thought. Maybe she never understood him the way he needed her to. It's not that he didn't love her, he did. Why was it so important for her to be married? Maybe, he should have told her he would have married her…eventually.

One of the most important things he learned from his father was to never let anything or anyone get in the way of success. But, in the quiet of his car, it was not his father's voice he continued to hear,

15

but her soft, teary voice, her words, "…and my career, my education, or my love for you has no importance to you?" Then he rested his head on the steering wheel and sobbed, because, although he knew she was right, he knew he would never turn back. Why? Because Trevour Scott has never turned back after walking out.

Chapter 3

"Scotty"

*S*cotty, *government name Trevour Edward Scott, III, grew up in a world of privilege. His mother's style of parenting wavered between authoritative and permissive, sadly more permissive than authoritative. His father, Major Trevour Edward Scott, Jr, who preferred to be called Eddie, was unaware his style of parenting was uninvolved, because his idea of being a good husband and father was to make sure there was enough bread on the table and in the bank. His presence was required at work in order to make those two things happened. This pleased Scottie's mother immensely and Scotty became accustomed to his dad not being available. In other words, unless something was really wrong, Scotty pretty much had his way and raised himself.*

Scotty's mother, who prefers being addressed as Professor Scott or Mrs. Scott, is a socialite and academic who teaches philosophy at one of the local universities. Her parents died when she was very young, and her life values derived from being raised by her socialite academic grandparents. It is evident her philosophy is that every child has the innate ability to make life decisions without much help from others, stemmed from how she was raised by her grandparents...hands off but within reach when needed.

Scotty's father came from a military family. His grandfather, Colonel T. E. Scott, Sr., who answers only to "Colonel," even by his family members, served in the United States Army for 46 years. He retired at age 64 and served as a circuit court judge until he was 72.

Scotty's grandmother was an Army Nurse. She served in the United States Army until she met the Colonel. When Scottie was born, she stayed with his parents for two years to help care for him until his mother recovered. In his mother's words, "Carting a human around inside of her body for nine months was bad enough, but then to go through the added trauma and pain of giving birth was too much." She made sure she would never have to endure this experience again, which is why Scottie is an only child.

Scotty's parents met while his father was in law school. His mother was a brand new philosophy professor. Although Scotty's parents met and married while his father was in the Army, his mother never adapted to military life. It interfered drastically with her aristocratic, down-with-the-government lifestyle. Although Scotty's father was raised in a military atmosphere himself, the military did not live in their home because his mother basically did not allow it. She "encouraged" her husband to be all that he could be, with whomever he needed to be it with, in the military, with two stipulations. Number one, the military stayed on the other side of the door. And number two, there will never be a discussion of divorce.

When home and with his family, Major Scott lived the aristocratic life his wife carved out for him. And so, until he retired from the Army, he traveled, without his family, and was not readily available to Scotty. Therefore, except for summer vacations and occasional family events, Scotty was on his own. His view on life was, whatever he wanted, he made happen on his own, so he thought.

Most of Scotty's academic life was spent in one boarding school or another. He was always excited when summer came because he would spend summers with his grandparents, regardless of where they were living at the time. At the beginning of the new school year he enjoyed bragging about where he spent the summer. His favorite vacation spot was Spain and Japan. One summer his father and grandfather were stationed in India together. Spending the summer with his dad and his grandmother was a memorable experience for him.

Scotty's grandmother was his only true love and the only true constant in his life. She was his moral compass. When he wandered out too far, she would be the one to reel him back to reality. Her death took him to a place that was hard for him to return from. His compass was gone and although he excelled in his military career, he was not so lucky in his personal relationships, especially when it came to love. Unfortunately, his grandmother died before she could teach him how to love and respect a woman while in a relationship. His parents and grandfather were there for him; however his mother's idea of love was materialistic, literally. Whatever she wanted she got. His father and grandfather showed him that taking care of family meant excelling in his career at the expense of family, or in his case the expense of every relationship he had...especially with Nattie.

It was never Scotty's father's intent to become a career Army lawyer and an absentee dad, but the only way to keep his wife happy was to stay away from her as much as possible while he was on active duty...her choice not his.

Scotty's Uncle Jack, Eddie's oldest brother, had already retired from the military and agreed to take on the responsibility of mentoring Scotty during his teenage years. Unfortunately for Scotty's father, his uncle became Scotty's go-to adult. Questions about any life issues he had were voiced to his uncle, not his father.

Eddie was an environmental lawyer, however while in the Army, his practice of law was basically whatever was needed at the time. Once retired, he was able to return to practicing law as an *environmental lawyer. He also became an advocate for laws to help prevent global warming and destruction of natural waterways and a lobbyist for various environmental causes, putting him on a path to politics. He ran a couple failed campaigns for senator before finally winning a seat as a state senator.*

This new career path continued to keep him away from home more than he liked. It saddened him that his wife still seemed to prefer him gone rather than at home. While he was trying to appease his wife, he neglected to see the even wider divide his career choices were making between him and his almost adult son.

Mrs. Scott continued to live in her world where teens should be allowed to learn to be responsible adults - naturally. It became apparent to everyone Scotty was not one of those teenagers becoming responsible "naturally" on his own. He finished his sophomore year of college with a 1.9 grade point average.

Senator Scott insisted Scotty join the military. He and Scotty's uncles knew the discipline, regiment and consistency of the military would be good for him. Scotty resisted, mainly because he felt his father had no right to tell him what to do since he wasn't around. To Scotty's surprise, his father agreed with him. He also reminded him that although he may not have been around physically, his money has been a constant, at least until now, because he would not continue to financially support Scotty's quest to fail in school or in life.

Although his mother did not like the idea of one more military/government employee in her family, she knew it was the best solution to what was becoming a serious situation. She could not have it said her son was academically challenged when he was not. And although rebelling has its place, now was not the time for him to act out when his father is active in politics and governmental affairs.

After some discussion with his uncle and the Army recruiter, and with much trepidation, Scotty agreed to enlist for four years and after his enlistment he would return to college to complete his degree.

As a philosopher, on many occasions, Mrs. Scott's evaluation of the government was less than stellar. Although she was proud to brag about her husband's career choices, she despised politics and at every opportunity took pleasure in debating any topic, with any politician, including her husband. She tolerated her husband's military career and now his government and political pursuits only because, in her circle, it gave her bragging rights as Mrs. Senator Trevour E. Scott, II.

Joining the Army turned out to be the best decision Scotty made to enhance his career. It taught him every discipline except one, how to love another person more than his career. That is one lesson the military could not teach him, especially since the Army is a very jealous and selfish lover. Unfortunately, neither his grandfather, nor his parents got around to showing him what a selfless relationship is supposed to look like.

Scotty's parents would tell him theirs was love at first sight and their relationship grew because they realized one very important fact early on in their marriage. Their personal and career interests, and how they pursued them, were the exact opposite of each other. However, their idea of financial and career stability was spot on. They taught Scotty that one makes their own way into a successful career and financial stability, and not only does the love of another person have nothing to do with it, but that love of another person should never, ever get in the way of career and financial success. Scotty's dad clearly used the Army and his law degree as a steppingstone to politics, and Scotty chose to follow in his dad's footsteps towards career and financial bliss.

Although his parents were constantly somewhere making money or making an appearance, sometimes together, most of the time separately, they did have family traditions and staples that kept them anchored. As a staple in the marriage, but also to keep up appearances, they scheduled "date night" that could not be changed except for family or national military emergency. They had family vacations twice a year. If his father, Eddie, was out of the area or even out of the country, if at all possible, he and his mother would travel to wherever his father was and that became their vacation. They attended required extended family events and took turns attending Scotty's school and social events.

Neither of Scotty's parents attended church regularly. His maternal grandparents were academics who did not discredit religion but, did not consider themselves religious. As a philosopher, Scotty's mother did not think it necessary to teach her son about a God, who in her opinion, was not logical. His father was raised in a semi-lackadaisical religious environment, meaning he was too busy in a war or in the courtroom for church. His grandmother went to church, but she was not an active member, meaning she was not a deaconess, or choir member, or usher, or any of the other things people in church needed to do to prove they were Christian.

So, as an adult, Scotty decided church wasn't necessary in order to believe there was a God; and a spiritual encounter was not required to be successful. He never understood how Nattie could turn on him, as she did, for an unseen God that had nothing to do with nothing…in his opinion.

And now, twenty years later, he is a successful Navy lawyer. He is very proud of his professional accomplishments. He has no regrets, except one, losing Nattie. Sometimes, during his quiet moments, he can hear her voice, her laughter, smell her perfume. Her smell was so unique, a mixture of coco butter and whatever perfume she decided to wear that day. Her favorite was Avon's Honeysuckle, Sweet Honesty and Candid. She loved her some Avon. I bought her Opium for her birthday, and she fell in love with it…not enough to get her away from Avon, but it was a start.

And now today, ever since he walked onto that train station platform, and smelled Opium, and saw that woman, he can't seem to get her out of his head. After all these years there are times he would think to himself, "I wonder what would have happened if I had just…". "Well, that's water under the bridge now. She had her opportunity to live in a world of luxury, just as my mother did, and she blew it for her God and her skimpy career. I've been all over the world and not run into her. I'll probably never run into her, especially not on a commuter train in Atlanta Georgia."

"So, why is she invading my thoughts, today…?"

Chapter 4

"Is This Really Happening?!"

*A*s Nancy ushered him into the conference room, Commander Scott is still bewildered as to what just happened.

"Nattie?" His head is spinning. How is it that I'm meeting with Nattie"? How did she get here? I mean, in this position. Will she be the barrier that could block my successful closing of this case...MY Nattie? When I left her she was a clerk...now she is...Dr....a doctor of what? And Morgan... who gave her that name, and where is he now. My meeting is with Nattie...my Nattie? After all of these years she just drops right back into my lap! Wouldn't that be nice. What a coincidence!"

He is so engrossed in the fact that it's her that he didn't realize he still had the Message Magazine in his hand from the waiting room. When he saw the magazine on the table it brought back so many memories, none good, mainly, because of him. He did not like the fact that he was being replaced by a church. Even he knew that wasn't the real reason he was so upset. He felt as if she had grown and no longer needed him as much as he thought she did in the beginning. He was so sure he would talk her into leaving the Navy to be with him, but obviously she didn't need him; obviously, she proved him wrong." Questions were whirling around in his head, "how will this work out?"

"Commander Scott, thank you for coming in." He stood. "Please sit. I'm curious as to why...?"

"Nattie..., I'm sorry, Dr. Morgan, please, before we get into business I'm still in shock that you are, first the train, and now here. I'm still trying to wrap my head around this. How have you been and what have you been doing all of these years? I still can't believe it's actually you!"

Hmm, Nattie thought, "I see he still likes interrupting people as they are talking." *I'm laughing inside and praying I'm not rolling my eyes as I sit.*

Oh what a much needed distraction, as Nancy walks in with tea, coffee and condiments. She always knows how to save the day.

"Thank you Nancy". *I was still laughing silently as I watched Scotty's entire countenance changed when Nancy walked in.* "Um yes, thank you."

He continues, "I am still in shock, running into you this morning and now realizing that I am meeting with you here." With what seemed to almost be a smirk, "This is a far cry from records keeping."

"Lucky for me, I learned lucrative skills while keeping records."

"Touché. So, what did you do after…"? His voice trailed off as his expression clearly revealed that he remembered.

I am not in the mood for reminiscing right now, especially with him. I want to know why he is here.

"Commander, now is not the time for reminiscing. You are here to discuss the GREENWOOD LAKE case, am I correct?"

"Um Nattie…well…yes, um…Dr. Morgan, you are correct. I am here to discuss the GREENWOOD LAKE. Where do you want to begin?"

"Commander, you made the appointment, so how about *you* begin."

He clearly has not learned to control his facial expressions as he realizes I am not in the mood for his cuteness; and I clearly intend to remain in control of this meeting. Too funny.

"Okay," as he squirms while opening his folder. "My office received a confidential, unofficial copy of a letter sent to your office on behalf of a sailor onboard USS GREENWOOD LAKE. The letter addresses actions he feels were inappropriately targeted towards him by members of his chain of command."

I'm wondering how did he get a copy of the letter? I chose not to interrupt him because I needed to know what he knew before my questions shut him down.

He continues, "We are concerned the information provided may just be the concerns of an over-protective mother and not the reality of what actually transpired."

"Commander, what do you mean by 'the reality of what actually transpired'. Do you feel the letter is fictious? Have you spoken to the mother or the client?"

"No Dr. Morgan, that is not what I'm saying. I, well we, just want to get to the bottom of this situation so that it can be resolved, as I'm sure you do as well."

"Am I to understand you came here before you spoke to Petty Officer Jackson nor his mother?

Am I detecting a little frustration here? I would really love to enjoy seeing him squirm, but I have to remember what is at stake here, the livelihood of a sailor who is not here to state his case.

"Commander, as I'm sure you know, the proper procedure is for this office to complete our investigation, compile and forward our recommendations to the commanding officer to resolve the issue. We have not sent our report to the command, and we did not ask your office to intervene, so please tell me why are you here?"

"Dr. Morgan, as you know, the responsibility of the legal office is to protect the command."

I'm trying not to be rude, but I am sitting here across from this man, remembering Scotty, remembering what he did, trying to wrap my head around why is he here, while seeing he is clearly trying to control this meeting and this case.

"I thought Sir, the responsibility of your office is to protect the truth. So, since you are here, out of order, how about we work together to find the truth."

"Dr. Morgan, the truth is, I am here, in an attempt, to resolve this situation as quickly as possible. The ship is preparing to get underway for an extensive at-sea exercise and will not have opportunity to give this case its due diligence. It has to be resolved now, preferably here."

"I have worked with the base legal office on several military cases. Please explain to me how you plan to resolve this case if you have not spoken to the source of the letter in order to access the true intentions of it?"

"Dr. Morgan..."

This time I interrupted him and pressed the intercom on the phone, "Nancy, do I have any time open tomorrow morning that can be blocked to work with Commander Scott on this case?"

After a moment Nancy replies, "No ma'am. You have court all morning, meetings until 3 p.m. and the event at 5 p.m. However, I can clear your schedule Thursday from 10 a.m. until 1 p.m."

"Thank you Nancy. Commander, is that time suitable for you?"

"Um, yes."

Commander Scott wanted to protest but he decided to save his energy for later.

"I had planned to be back in Norfolk on Thursday, but yes ma'am, that will be fine. I am not due in court, so I will have my office reschedule my appointments."

I slowly stood up and held my hand out. "Thank you sir, we will reconvene on Thursday. We will provide brunch. Nancy will see you out."

Commander Scott responded almost in a haze, "Um, thank you, um no, I can find my way. Um, thank you again for meeting with me at such short notice."

As he walked out, I felt the need to cry unto the Lord for STRENGTH! My goodness! I remember him in his Army dress uniform. Nothing I remember compares to him in his Navy Summer Whites, looking as good going out as he did coming in. Oh my goodness! But I had to keep my composure and I guess Nancy's composure as well!

"Nancy!"

"I'm sorry Doc, was my inside voice showing on my outside face?! I forgot for a moment...**MER-CEE!** Oh, and by the way Doc, your inside voice is **ALL OVER** your outside face too. Ha!"

I gave her that raised eyebrow look, "Never mind Nancy! We have work to do."

"Yes Ma'am!" *Nancy smiled and peeked down the hall for another glance.*

As Commander Scott rode down the elevator he was talking out loud, "What just happened! Did she just dismiss me, again. Is she trying to derailed my plan?"

But, for however long it was he stood there, the only thing he could really think about was could he really prosecute this case against Nattie, while his brain is wondering what would have been if...

Now, today, he has to pull himself together to do the job he was sent here to do. Just because it's Nattie...what difference should that make? Again out loud, "I'm the best prosecutor on the east coast, probably in the entire Navy legal system. I got this! ... I hope!?" *However, his inside voice was all over his outside face too because he never thought he would ever see her again and now that he has...what now?*

Chapter 5

Tuesday, September 14, 1999, 4 p.m.

"Missing Him Tears – UGH!"

*A*fter Commander Scott left I sat on the couch in my office, trying to relax. Tracy would be here shortly to pick me up for our dinner and movie date. I need to be calm and relaxed for him. I feel in order to get myself together, I need some good old mid-watch coffee, thick and bitter, tainted with a tablespoon of Hennessy, for medicinal purposes of course, and a ten-minute power nap. Then **maybe,** I will be able to recover from *who* just happened. I prayed there were no more walk-ins or phone calls from anyone, not even the congresswoman. But, unfortunately, what did invade my mind was …

New Year's Day

January 1ˢᵗ, 1980

"Diary – I read someplace that whatever is happening in your life on New Year's Day is an indication of the road your life will travel for the rest of the year. If that is true, my 1980 is doomed. I am mad as a hornet. I hurt beyond words, because I allowed myself to love and be loved… to what end. I am mad because I let myself be vulnerable, when maybe I should not have. I am mad because I love Scotty and how long will it be before I can honestly say the words "loved" and "Scotty" in the same sentence without hating him, knowing I shouldn't because he showed me himself before last night. I saw the "real" him during those times when it was clear that he was only concerned about himself and his future. I was just another link he needed in his bracelet to move forward. And to think, I gave him that bracelet…UGH! It took him reminding me that love has nothing to do with it. And now, I'm back to where I started. The only man that truly loved me was Michael, and right now, I'm doubting that. I have not received any word from him, not even a postcard, for a very long time. I can't be angry at Michael. He told me he was not forever. Scotty is not his fault. Scotty is my fault.

Well, at least my girlfriends came over to comfort me. I called Janice in tears. She called the others and they were here within minutes. We ate food, drank spirits, played spades, and laughed while we did some serious man bashing. They wanted to sleep over so I wouldn't be alone, but I assured them I would be fine. We will have lunch today. But right now Diary I lied, because last night I told you I had no tears left for him and that tomorrow would begin a new year and the beginning of a new life for me. Well, today is tomorrow and I am incredibly sad, and now, I have "missing him" tears. Maybe, I should have gone after him. Maybe, I should find him and tell him I'll try to get orders near him. Maybe…maybe I should just call a spade a spade and forget he ever existed. UGH! God, this is horrible. I really don't want to miss him, but I do. Diary, you have always been my silent therapist. Thank you."

And now, twenty years later, I am exhausted, and I have a migraine, because of all of these uninvited memories and because they reappeared in person… JESUS! WHY!? I'm going to need a real therapist.

I have to admit, looking back, Scotty did me a favor that night. Once I realized I would survive, for real, I had a wonderful life, and, an extremely rewarding Navy career, which put me in the direct path of my current position. I met a wonderful man and had a great marriage, for a season.

At first, the breakup with Scotty was difficult, actually, devastating. I traveled aimlessly and mechanically through the seven stages of grief, not really knowing how I would survive or how to snap out of it. There were days when I was so angry with Scotty, I wished I had thrown him out the window when I had the chance. There were somedays I was angry with myself because I was angry with him. Fortunately, I did not spend too much time blaming God, because I knew He had nothing to do with how ugly Scotty had become.

I could see the selfishness in him coming out more and more long before that dreadful night. I thought I had prepared myself, but I hadn't. Although there were no more heart-hurt tears left for him, there were many anger-tears and depression-tears and why-me-tears, and … just tears. For a couple years, in danger was the man that tried to come across my path. How I managed to remain professional and successful at work still boggles my mind because my personal life was a dark pit with slick walls. I tried not to forget God would never leave me nor forsake me, but it was hard. I tried not to forget where my help came from, but that was just as hard. So I waddled in my misery with that happy face mask you see on cartoons. Nobody knew how much I hurt. Nobody knew how unsafe I really was. In the 70s and 80s going to see a therapist was out of the question if you wanted to remain employed by the Navy. Instead, I found solace in substances. Sometimes the substance was liquid, sometimes it was plants and sometimes it was a pen and paper. And then one day I remembered who my Help was when I happened to see an old Message Magazine with hills on the cover with Jesus *standing at the top with His arms open. The text was Psalms 121:1-2… "I will lift up mine eyes unto the hills, from whence cometh my help. My help cometh from the Lord, which made heaven and earth." That's when I decided I did not have to stay in that pit, slick walls or no slick walls, because I had help. I went back to church, met great friends who are still an intricate part of my life today…and I met the man that became my forever husband and the father of my boys.*

So, all in all, Scotty did me a favor. He taught me I can survive stabbing hurt and with God's help, create a very successful life and career for myself, in and out of the Navy.

I never thought I would see him again, especially in a Navy uniform. Very seldom do you see military who have crossed services. I wonder how did that happen. Ugh, why do I care. I never thought God would allow such a catastrophe to invade my life again. Now that he is back, God I'm depending on you to see me through.

Chapter 6

I woke up this morning with my mind, stayed on Jesus.

I woke up this morning with my mind, stayed on Jesus.

I woke up this morning with my mind, stayed on Jesus.

Hallelu – Hallelu – Hallelu-jah…

I don't know why this song woke me up this morning. It had to be the angels singing to me because I had already hit the snooze on the radio, so it was not on the radio, must have been the angels. I know that demon angel is trying to find ear plugs, but they better be good, because the angels are singing LOUD, and this song is in my head to stay.

Tracy and I had a wonderful evening. He was gone on assignment and returned yesterday. He told me what he could about his trip, without of course, having to kill me. Even though I still have a high level federal government security clearance, I am, unfortunately, a civilian and I am not privy to most Navy secrets. Sometimes I can read between the lines and sometimes I don't try. There are things about my job that, even with his high-powered clearance, he is not privy too, so I guess we are even in that respect. So, he told me what he could, and I told him what I could, including the appearance of uninvited memories. Shortly after we met, I told him about Scotty while we were comparing love-tragedy notes. He declared that my love-tragedy topped all of his. Ha!Ha!

Lieutenant Tracy and I met because of a case I had that brought me to the Navy base. He was new to his position as chief of security and new to Atlanta. The first thing that caught my eye was those beautiful white teeth that lit up the room when he smiled. He was seated when I walked into his office and as he stood, I felt as if I was looking at a fifteen story chocolate skyscraper!

We became acquainted while working on a particular case involving a sexual harassment issue between a civilian woman (Alice) and a military man (Jones). Alice mailed a letter of complaint to Jones' Command Master Chief, however, it mysteriously showed up in our office. At the conclusion of the investigation it was discovered Alice had not been sexually harassed. She eventually admitted the encounters were consensual and she was angry because Jones was also having consensual encounters with a military woman (Brenda) he worked with. It was further discovered the complaint reached our office because another military woman (Susan) was angry because he did not consent to having consensual encounters with her. To ensure an investigation would be opened, Susan mailed a copy of the letter to our office. It was a total waste of the Navy's time and resources, as well as my office's time and resources. Needless to say all parties, including Alice, found themselves in very hot water.

The good thing for me was I offered my services as a tour guide for Lieutenant Tracy. That was three years ago. The sad part is, he will be transferring soon to Italy for a new assignment. Everyone with firsthand experience in the Navy knows sailors come and sailors go. And if you fall in love with one it's your responsibility to accept it because that's just how it is done.

Right now, my reality is the hectic day I have today, so there is no time to become all misty-eyed and puffy faced. Nor do I have time to stand in front of my closet waiting, once again, for a dress to reach out and touch me. One of these days, I'm going to take on the strategy of my ex and pick out, on Sunday, what I'm going to wear the entire week, Monday – Friday for work and what to wear on Sabbath. What a concept! Ha! One of these days…but obviously not today. Maybe, if I call and tell him I need help organizing my clothes for the week he might come back. Ha! Ha! Nope.

I feel like purple today...that will work.

In the mist of everything else going on in my office, I have to be feet deep in this investigation on the GREENWOOD LAKE case. I told Nancy she could put everything else that's not urgent to the side to start researching the ship and the family. I still have an icky feeling about this case...like there's a very big and important piece missing; and I can't help but wonder if Commander Scott has that piece.

Commander Scott...Lord, what are you trying to tell me? I know he is here to defend the ship, but again I am asking You, **"WHAT IS HE DOING HERE!?"** And more importantly Lord, how should I handle this case. You are really going to have to help me on this one, **FOR REAL!"**

As soon as I opened the door of the Coffee Shoppe Sally stuck a mug of Earl Grey in my face.

"Sally!...What...UGH! Were you standing at the door waiting for me to appear! Thank you for the tea because yes I need this right now, but my goodness, could you have let me get in the door first!"

"Yes Ma'am I was waiting for you! It wasn't hard. You come about the same time every morning." As soon as I was completely in the shop, Mr. Peterson called out to me, "Na'tal-lee how are you, are you okay? You didn't need for me to handle anything for you? I sat by my phone waiting for you to call!"

"Good morning Mr. Peterson, there is nothing to handle. I'm doing fine. How are Mr. Tibbs and Ms. Valerie doing?"

Sally chimes in again, "Soooo, how was the rest of your day yesterday?"

"Sally, aren't there other people in need of coffee this morning?"

"Jeanet'te is taking care of them. So ...?"

"Merciful Mercy! Have you been dreaming about the possibilities of what may have happened, Ms. Sally?"

Sally laughing, "Yes!"

"When we left here, he went his way, and I went my way. And to be honest, yes, seeing Scotty, in the flesh, brought back all kinds of memories and emotions, all of which were uninvited."

"So, are you going to see him to catch up...?"

Before Sally could complete her thought or I could respond, Mr. Peterson responded, almost shouting, which we have never heard him do, **"OF COURSE NOT!** Tracy will not like that at all and neither will I, if you want to know the truth of the matter. I do not like this Scotty person. There is something shady about him. **I don't like him at all!"**

Pastor Bannister was sitting sipping his coffee trying to figure out what happened. "What is going on, if I might ask?". Before anyone could say a word, Ms. soon-to-be-a lawyer-chatterbox Sally said, "Pastor, these last couple days were not the days for you to have missed being here! It all started on Monday when Nattie thought she saw someone that looked like an old Navy lover...I mean boyfriend...sorry, Mr. Peterson, from when she first joined the Navy and..."

"SALLY!" Nattie halted her in mid-breath. "Sally, may I please tell my own story?" With an exasperated sigh Sally replied, "Only if you promise to tell the whole truth and nothing but the whole truth. Otherwise I will have to fill in the blanks as I see fit. As you know I'm in law school with a 4.0 grade point average, so, I know how to do that!" She laughed.

Nattie sighed and shook her head, "Pastor, as Sally said, what I thought was an uninvited memory became a reality yesterday morning when an acquaintance from my past appeared before me in the flesh, here in the shop. His name is Trevour Scott, III. He and I dated for several years when I was stationed in Washington, DC during my first tour, twenty years ago. Needless to say, it was a shock seeing him again and being flooded with all those memories, good and bad." I smiled, "Mr. Peterson was my champion, ready to draw blood, if necessary, to defend my honor."

"Anyway, Mr. Peterson, unfortunately, I will have no choice but to see him again, maybe several agains."

"What do you mean, see him?" *Mr. Peterson slumped his shoulders and sighed as if I were his teenage daughter telling him I'm pregnant,* "What about…?"

"Mr. Peterson, I told Tracy everything last night. He already knew the story of Scotty, and last night I told him about Scotty's appearance. But there is more. I'm working on a Navy discrimination case that I planned to talk to Pastor Bannister about and it turns out that Scotty is now a Navy Commander and a lawyer; and he is in Atlanta because of the same case. He came to my office yesterday afternoon not knowing he would be meeting with me."

You could hear a pin drop. Sally stood there with no words, which has never happened since I've known her. Even the other customers were now all in my story. I wanted to choke Sally for bringing it up in front of company. I thought I had taught that child better. I'm really gonna have to have a talk with her. She is going to make a great lawyer because she does not mind sticking other people's neck out there to be chopped off.

Mr. Peterson sat with a very puzzled face, "I don't understand, did he know yesterday morning you were the one he would be meeting with and just pretended he was surprised to see you? I tell you I don't like him one bit!"

"Right now, Mr. Peterson, I don't think he knew he was meeting with me. When he knew me I was still using my maiden name so he had no way of knowing I was the one he would be meeting. I'm still trying to piece together the reason for him showing up to my office unannounced; however, when he saw me in my office it was clear he was extremely surprised."

"Hum...," Mr. Peterson responded making it plain he wasn't buying it at all.

My train is pulling in. Sally brought me another cup of tea to go, "So what now?"

I paused and shrugged. "It's a case, I'll treat it like any other case. And I have to pray for discernment about what to do about the case and about Commander Scott."

Mr. Peterson responded, "That's for sure and I will be asking the Virgin Mary to help you see what's what!"

"Pastor Banister, I really need your help on this case. May I call you later to discuss it?"

"Of course," he replied. "Call me after one o'clock. I should be in my office by then. I have a funeral this morning."

"Thank you. I will be in court off and on today, so I will call in this afternoon as soon as I get a break."

Mr. Peterson's face was still scrunched up, "Mr. Peterson I promise you I will be fine. I will see you all tomorrow. Be blessed and have a great day."

As I boarded the train I had an overwhelming desire to go back home, crawl back in my bed and sleep until tomorrow. However, that would be a very bad idea since I need every moment I'm not in court today to investigate this case. I have to be prepared to meet with Commander Scott tomorrow morning.

I think I will read a little bit and try to relax before this workday starts.

I'm walkin' and talkin' with my mind, stayed on Jesus.

I'm walkin' an talkin' with my mind, stayed on Jesus.

I'm walkin' and talkin' with my mind, stayed on Jesus.

Hallelu – Hallelu – Hallelu-jah...

Chapter 7

Thursday, September 16, 1999

"Meeting 2: Poker Faces"

*C*ommander Scott arrived promptly at ten o'clock to start work on the case. "Good Morning Nancy, aren't you looking beautiful this morning? Good morning Nat...um Dr. Morgan. You are still an unexpected and gorgeous surprise."

Nancy looked at me with that "I'm glad I wore boots today" sideways glance. I'm sure I had that *'Wow, really...it's too early in the morning!?'* look on my face, as well.

There was a time, when I was a different girl, that pearly white smile would melt my heart, my mind and my spirit. That girl no longer exist and this woman is not falling in the syrup.

Last night I told Tracy about my interaction with Commander Scott. He agreed that it was not normal protocol for a representative from the base legal office to just pop up without an invitation from the congressional official investigating the case. He and I both wondered if the commanding officer was trying to circumvent the process because there is something to hide. Or maybe Mr. Peterson's instincts are right…maybe Commander Scott came to Atlanta with ulterior motives.

"Good morning Commander, I'm glad to see you are well and ready to get to work. Nancy will show you to the conference room. There is coffee and snacks there for your convenience."

"Thank you Dr. Morgan."

The annoyed look on his face would have been undetectable by someone else, but I saw it. I smiled as I disappeared into my office. I needed a moment to pray and get myself together. "Lord, I need your strength and your power right now because I still don't understand why he is here AND he is still not fat with brown teeth!"

After an hour of pushing paper back and forth between Nancy, Commander Scott and I, it was evident we were getting nowhere. As in any good poker game we all held our cards close to our chest and put on our best poker faces. I really felt he was fishing to see where we were headed. We all came to the conclusion there was more to the story than what was in the letter. So basically, after turning papers this way and that way, we were no closer to the truth than before we started.

"Commander Scott, I think we have exhausted all the resources we have available to us on this table. As I mentioned to you Tuesday this office has not completed its investigation; and it seems your office still has work to do as well."

"Dr. Morgan, I understand I jumped the gun, so to speak; however, I...well, my office has its reasons for getting to the bottom of this case as soon as possible."

"Commander Scott, you could have sent a letter or called, so, my question to you is why would a lawyer from Atlantic Fleet come to Atlanta concerning this case?" *Commander Scott did not respond at once. It was obvious he was choosing his words very carefully.*

"Dr. Morgan, I appreciate you indulging me by meeting to see if we have common ground concerning this case. However, I sense your words might be laced with just a little bit of suspicion. I assure you my motives concerning this case are above board. Once it was known your office had a letter from the crewmember's mother, the ship legal officer asked my advice on how to handle the matter. Someone from your end sent a copy of the letter to the GREENWOOD LAKE. He asked if I would personally investigate this matter. Since I had to come to Atlanta on a personal matter, I said I would come to talk to the investigator. To tell you the truth, I'm still in shock that you are the investigator and I feeling a little out of my element."

Nancy and I looked at each other bewildered, "What do you mean by *someone from this end*?"

"We received a copy of the letter from a private citizen who wanted to remain anonymous, literally. No signature or return address. "

"Commander, why did you not mention all of this the other day? There would have been no reason…"

Suddenly I could hear Mr. Peterson's warnings. Did he withhold this information on purpose so he could come back here today? The same question was on Nancy's face…

"…there would have been no reason for us to meet knowing we had no information to work with. Why was it important that you return this morning?"

Although she really wanted to hear his response, Nancy decided this was the perfect time for her to get coffee or sharpen pencils or any other little task to get herself out of the room.

"Lunch is being delivered. I will go downstairs to meet the deliverer. They should be here any moment," *said Nancy as she stood up. I did not want to be left alone with him. Right now I am trying to be diplomatic despite I am spitting nails mad!*

"I did not know I was meeting with *you*. When I saw you I kinda lost my train of thought. I knew I was babbling, so when you recommended meeting this morning, it worked for me. It gave me an opportunity to wrap my head around you being here and on this case. I did not think how or when we received the letter was that big of a deal. People mail us and commanding officers all the time when they are upset about something. I'm sure you ran across a letter or two while on active duty. How long did you stay in? I'm sure not long, right?"

I tried not to frown, but how dare he think I didn't notice he did not answer my question and now he is trying to change the subject. And what does that mean..."not long, right?"

"Twenty-two and a half years."

The look on his face was priceless. I had to smile.

"What?! Really?! I know you said you planned to stay in, but I didn't think you would. Twenty-two and a half years. Impressive. So you retired as an officer? You could have stayed in much longer."

Smile gone just that quick, "I retired as a Navy Counselor Chief Petty Officer, with a Master's Degree in Counseling and half of my PhD in Psychology."

Ahhhh, that's the look I wanted to see on his face. Utter astonishment..

"I was onboard the USS Shenandoah when she decommissioned. I was the Ship's Counselor."

"Wait." Scotty stood up and walked towards the window. He turned to look at Nattie scratching his head."

"I was at Norfolk Naval Base at that time, and I worked with the decommissioning of the ship. How is it we never crossed paths?"

I couldn't help but smile, "Karma I'm sure."

He laughed, "You still have that 'icy-cut-to-the-bone' sense of humor I see."

With a raised eyebrow I responded, "Back to our original conversation, Commander Scott, why are you here?"

He smiled. Why did he smile? He still has a beautiful smile…UGH!!!

"Nattie I…" *The conference room phone rang.*

"Dr. Morgan speaking. Really?…Really?!…Just cancel it…Sure, no problem, that will be fine. Thank you…Have a nice day." *Dialing another number,* "I'm sorry Commander I'll just be a moment. Hello, yes this is Dr. Morgan. Is Nancy there with you? … Yes please. Nancy, the caterer called to say the lunch would not be delivered for another hour. I canceled the order…Yes, that's fine. I'll see you later."

"I'm sorry Commander, it seems the restaurant had an issue and our lunch won't be ready for another hour. I feel we have accomplished all we can today, don't you? Nancy is gone to run a couple errands because we have a very busy afternoon ahead of us, as I'm sure you do also. I'm sorry lunch fell through."

There he goes, smiling again. "Not necessarily. I would be honored if you would allow me to take you out to lunch. You can choose the restaurant."

Every voice in my head, especially Mr. Peterson's, was screaming, "NO!! Don't do it! It's a trick!" One voice quietly said, "You didn't eat breakfast, so you need to eat a little something. Go to The Southside Deli. You got this!"

"There's a deli within walking distance. That would be nice, thank you. However, lunch is on me since we were planning to treat you anyway."

Scotty just sat there for a moment, as if he did not hear her response. Then, the smile AGAIN. I'm saying to myself pray without ceasing…just pray without ceasing.

Chapter 8

The Case...

We received a letter insinuating harassment and possible discrimination involving the religious liberty of a sailor who works in the ship engineering department. The letter also insinuated the sailor's request for an officer program has been hindered.

The harassment started after a new sailor came onboard to work in his department. The letter stated, he was not getting support from his superiors regarding the harassment, including mismanagement of his request to apply for an officer program.

The final paragraph in her letter read, *"...I'm writing this letter on my own. My son did not ask me to write you. I know he will endure continued harassment and mistreatment until he is transferred or something terrible happens..."*

The Defendants...

Engineman First Class John Harvey, United States Navy

While reviewing Petty Officer Harvey's records, I found something very interesting. Petty Officer Harvey and Petty Officer Jackson shared the same birth date…ten years apart. And they were both exposed to working on engines at a young age. So I wonder if Petty Officer Harvey's fears stem from the fact that not only does he see his career slowly dying, but also that he sees his life being overrun by adolescents.

John Robert Harvey was born on September 23rd, 1963, in Natchez, Mississippi. Mississippi was still quite segregated at that time and if it were left up to most Mississippi residents it would have remained segregated. Growing up, John did not think it strange, in the late 60s and early 70s, to see non-white people walking on or moving to whatever side of the street white people were not walking on. He did not think it strange that there were still white only and black only signs everywhere and the Klu Klux Klan made the rules. He did not think it strange he went to an all-white school and an all-white church…whenever they went to school or church because his family owned a farm and farming was more important than school or church.

John was an average boy. He did not grow up in the city of Natchez. He grew up in a community of farmers. His parents grew a variety of vegetables and raised animals for the purpose of being sold at the farmer's market and to local stores. He and his brothers raised pigs to be sold at the market; however, once or twice a year they were able to raise one or two hogs to show at the local and state fair. On several occasions he or one of his brothers won ribbons for their show hogs. People came from near and far to purchase his mother's preserved fruits and vegetables. With all of that they were considered an average family, one, maybe two bad seasons from being destitute.

He hated school but was an average student. He was neither athletic nor scholastic. He liked working on engines. On the farm he was responsible for making sure the equipment worked properly. If his father had to hire someone to fix a piece of equipment he was angry with John for not fixing it. On one occasion John was severely injured because he was trying to fix the brakes on a tractor. After the accident his mother made his father pay for someone to fix the larger machinery.

In high school he went to school half days for academics and to the vocational school the remaining half of the day learning to work on engines. When he graduated from high school he worked the farm with his family for about six months and decided it wasn't for him anymore. The day he came home to announce he had enlisted into the Navy was the last day his father spoke to him.

EN1 Harvey arrived at the GREENWOOD LAKE angry. He tolerated the Navy and the Navy tolerated him. He served seventeen years with nothing much to show for it. He has been passed over for promotion to many times. And this year he was not recommended for promotion. He has one more opportunity to submit his request for advancement. If he is not promoted he will be forced to retire from the Navy with twenty years of service as a first class petty officer.

Retiring as a first class petty officer is not a sin nor a disgrace to any sailor. Many sailors with impeccable records don't get selected to continue in the Navy as a Chief Petty Officer. And there are some selected with very questionable career records. The selection is based on many aspects of a sailor's career, but more importantly, the needs of the Navy at the time of selection. Sometimes sailors are passed over because they missed an important qualification or certification in their field. Sometimes they are passed over because of some indiscretion that continues to haunt them every time they apply for advancement. And sometimes the only reason they were passed over is because the Navy only needed 30 promotions in their field and so sailors numbers 31 and over did not make the cut.

In the case of EN1 Harvey, the number of qualifying boxes checked were overshadowed by the number of boxes not checked. At every command, especially when on sea duty, it seemed drama always surrounded him...resembling the aftermath of a tornado...damage and destruction everywhere you look. Of course, whatever the drama was, it wasn't because of him. It was always because of something someone else did or did not do. When his discretions warranted some sort of severe repercussions there always seemed to be a loophole he could slide through to save himself. His supervisors always wondered how he ever lasted so long in the Navy. How was it he managed to literally slide alongside a court-martial board but never ending up in front of one? One of his prior chiefs told the chief on the GREENWOOD LAKE to be aware of him at all times. Why? He was about as slippery as an oiled-down pig. His performance evaluations are mediocre, resembling an exam where the test taker marked all Cs just so it can be said he completed the exam. He always passed his physical readiness test, and he showed up for work on time almost every day. He completed solitary tasks with no problem; however, he was not a team player, and he was not team leader material. Since he had been on the GREENWOOD LAKE, almost a year, his track record had not improved much. However, he still hoped for a supervisory position. In his eyes, once they made him a supervisor, then he would be able to prove himself to all of them.

Harvey's big break finally came when the leading petty officer (LPO) in his division received transfer orders a year early. This was the break he needed because, by seniority, he was the next in line for the position. By default he could finally slip through a loophole and automatically become the next leading petty officer. He always felt his previous ships dealt him a shovel full of misfortune. He felt his previous chief didn't like him and didn't want him to be the leading petty officer. Actually, he knew his chief didn't like him because he was the first one to disapprove his request for advancement. Harvey refused to admit in every situation and on every ship, he was ineligible because he was mediocre in his duties.

You would think, since he has been onboard over a year, his goal would have been to prove he was ready for a leadership position.

You would think his first order of business would have been to complete whatever work related qualifications he has not completed.

You would think his first order of business would have been to familiarize himself with the duties of a leading petty officer in his division, in port and underway.

You would think his first order of business would have been to start qualifications and prepare to test for Enlisted Surface Warfare Specialist, which, although may not be required, is expected of anyone wanting a supervisory position.

You would think his first order of business would have been to get acquainted with the other First Class Petty Officers on the ship and with his department personnel.

You would think any number of career enhancing actions would be on his list of things to do immediately.

Instead, EN1 Harvey's first order of business was to clip the wings of a certain petty officer, Engineman Second Class

Philipe Reece Jackson whom the department leaders were grooming for an officer's program, and if that didn't pan out, there would be a possibility he would be considered for the leading petty officer position. Why? Because Jackson is Mr. Joe Sailor and everyone thinks he knows everything about everything. He has been nothing less than a thorn in EN1 Harvey's side from the first day, and Harvey decided he was not about to let Jackson cheat him out of his right to become the new leading petty officer. Instead of Harvey using his energy to show himself worthy as a leader, he made it his duty to knock Jackson down a couple pegs. They all needed to see Jackson wasn't their Golden Boy.

Engineman Second Class (SW) Philipe Reece Jackson, United States Navy

While compiling information about EN2(SW) Jackson the first thing that jumped right in front of my face was the fact he was born the same year I graduated from high school, almost to the day. Geez Louise these sailors are getting younger and younger. I knew the day would come when there would be babies joining the Navy. Ha! Ha! I remember my Chief saying they were already in the Navy when I was born and if I live long enough…! Praise God I lived long enough!. Ha!Ha!

Philipe was the youngest of four children until a "surprise", as his parents describe it, came along in the form of his baby sister, Jeanne, who entered the world when he was three years old. They were all Navy Brats, growing up on or near a Navy base, with their own personalized seabags, transferring every three or four years right alongside their parents. Philipe' was born in the middle of his father's enlistment in Rota Spain, and he lived in states and countries his high school friends had only read about in books, like Spain, Louisiana, Japan, Hawaii and Australia. His parents made sure they were able to visit as much of the state or country they lived in as possible. They also went on vacation to Guam, the Philippines and South Korea. While in Spain they visited everywhere the train would take them.

Philipe was considered the middle child because his oldest brother is seven years older than him, his brothers directly above him (by three years) are twins who, most of the time, were treated as one child, then him and finally his sister, Jeanne. As the middle child, Philipe learned early on to make sure there was a back-up and a substitute plan for every situation. He learned to entertain himself and, as a result, had a very adventurous childhood. He enjoyed reading and visiting the local library whenever possible. This led to being "familiar" with equal amounts of information with substance and nonsense. It was not uncommon for him to say to anyone standing still long enough to hear something along the lines of, "Do you know the difference between molecules and atoms? Well, first of all there is no such thing as a molecule without atoms because molecules are a combination of two or more atoms via chemical bonding. However (pointing his index finger in the air as a symbol of knowledge) an atom is an individual chemical species which, when combined with each other, form molecules. And then he waits to see how long it takes for them to "get it". The "it" being he just said the same thing two different ways. Or, on a lighter note he might say, "Dad, in Georgia (where is dad is from) the use of a fork is illegal when eating what food? Answer, Fried Chicken! (which by the way should be illegal in every state!)" Then he would fall out laughing! And sometimes he would even say while doubled over with laughter, "Man I crack myself up!" His dad would just shake his head and go back to whatever he was doing.

Being a military brat has its advantages and obstacles. How many children literally get to travel all over the world because of their parents' job. He had "civilian" friends whose parents traveled while they stayed with grandparents. Some hardly knew their parents, which was sad. And some parents and their children have never been outside of the city they live in.

As the youngest boy, Philipe was the proud recipient of the handed-down, handed-down and handed-down again, hand-me-downs. Lucky for him, by the time shirts and pants got to him they were only good for play clothes and yard work. Praise God he didn't have to wear them to school or church to be teased into oblivion by every child within a hundred-mile radius. He was also blessed that his brothers never allowed a pair of shoes, dress or sneakers to last long enough for him to have to wear them. It wasn't that their parents were "poor;" with five children, four of them growing boys, they had to be resourceful with every dollar. Consequently, they were able to support their children through college and young adulthood. They taught them to enjoy life without being foolish with their money.

Philipe and his sister learned many lessons of what was and was not acceptable in the eyes of their parents and God by watching their older brothers continually be "court-marshalled" for one offense or another. Needless to say, living in a military family, with his father away a lot, his mother had many creative ways to reinforce positive behavior in her children.

Philipe's disciplinary actions occurred mainly because he had not learned how to control his face from telling his mother what his inside voice was saying. Or he would think he was using his inside voice, when in reality, he was using his outside voice. Also, he sometimes forgot that being the cute little baby boy was not always the ticket out of every situation.

One of his mother's tools of discipline was to make them memorize bible verses that she felt spoke to whatever the offense was. She would make them memorize the verse, write an essay about the verse and how it pertains to whatever they did, and then present it to the family. If nothing else, the result was they were a force to be reckoned with during Bible Bowl Tournaments, they always got A's on essay questions in school and were able to debate about almost anything. However, when all else failed, she would quote Proverbs 13:24 (NIV): *"Whoever spares the rod hates their children, but the one who loves their children is careful to discipline them."* Then, they knew they were in big trouble and there would be sad faces in the house that day.

As an adult Philipe is still referred to as the "runt" of the family because he is the youngest boy and because he is several "nots." He is not tall like his dad, or brothers and, he is not a jock like his brothers, which stressed out the men folk in his entire family. His oldest brother received a full scholarship to West Point where he played football for the entire four years leading to a promising future in the Army and the NFL. His twin brothers were athletic in one sport or the other during high school and college. One of his twin brothers joined the Air Force as a pilot. The other twin brother broke tradition and did not join the military and became a special education teacher. His sister, Jeanne, now a freshman in high school, enjoys gymnastics and swimming, so they are just waiting to see where she wants to go with it. His mother was proud of all of her children's successes; however, she enjoyed having someone to talk to about something other than sports. Also, he was not messy, like his twin brothers, which stressed him out because they were always leaving something where it did not belong.

Philipe was an excellent student, kindergarten through 12th grade. All things mathematics, science and gadgets fascinated him. He was the child that enjoyed his toys **AFTER** he had taken them apart and put them back together again.

He was the child everyone brought their broken things to. He enjoyed working on engines with his dad and it was not surprising that he decided, at a very young age, to follow in his father's footsteps by becoming a mechanical engineer. He not only loved the mechanics of engines, but he was also fascinated by the science of engines...*why* what made them tick was just as important as the ticking. In high school and college, he excelled in his science, technology, engineering and math (STEM) classes. While in high school he completed one year of college level basic general studies and engineering credits. Once in college, it was very easy for him to complete his Engineering Associate Degree. Although he completed two years of Navy Reserve Officer Training Corps (NROTC) in high school, he was in community college before he seriously considered the Navy as a career choice. Once in the Navy he excelled in engineering as an engineman. The reason he chose engineman is because he would be able to work on diesel engines used for ship propulsion, electrical power generation and other services such as oil, water and air piping systems, maintaining the ship's main engines, auxiliary boilers and other auxiliary machinery including steering engines, elevators, pumps and many other responsibilities.

He felt comfortable with his career choice, especially after receiving the approval of his father and brother.

He took his oath of enlistment and after completing bootcamp and Engineman School he reported to his first ship, in Pearl Harbor, Hawaii. He felt as if he was going home. It was a good duty station. After four years he transferred to Norfolk, Virginia. Normally, a sailor would rotate between sea and shore duty, however, EN2 Jackson asked for the USS GREENWOOD LAKE because it was one of the ships his father was assigned to. He felt honored to serve on the same ship as his father. Even though this ship is newer, with a newer engine, his father, now a long-time retired sailor shed a tear or two when Philipe showed him is orders. Even retired Salty Sailors get sentimental sometimes.

Chapter 9

*D*ear Diary, you and I have been together for a very long time. We have had all kinds of adventures. I know there were days when you silently cringed at some of the things I've taken out of my head and wrote them on your pages so that you could help me make logic out of it. I thank you for being my confidant and secret keeper for all of these years. I have encouraged everyone to start a journal.

You have been with me through all of the tears, through all of the seasons. I thought that when I retired and settled here, I would be done with "a time to tear and a time to mend; a time to be silent and a time to speak; a time to love and a time to hate." (Ecclesiastes 3:7-8a NIV), with things in and out of season.

Well, I'm back to counting months, weeks, days, and hours because he is slowly becoming out of season. He has orders to a far-away land and more than likely I will never see him again. Well, I *guess I shouldn't say never since Scotty showed up what...20 years later. What the world!!! UGH! Why??? Okay, I don't want to think about him right now. It's bad enough that I have to endure him through this case. I don't want him invading my personal thoughts as well.*

As I was saying, before more Scotty memories rudely invade my thoughts, I will not erase my Lieutenant from my memories, but I know better than to expect a long distance anything from either of us. We had a wonderful evening and I'm looking forward to seeing him this weekend. Unfortunately, I will be traveling next week.

Speaking of traveling, I suppose I should sleep because tomorrow I make preparations to travel to Norfolk to visit the USS GREENWOOD LAKE. This is one adventure I am not looking forward to. However, on the bright side, I'll get to walk around a real Naval Base, go to the Navy Exchange and Commissary. Yes, I know I have access to the commissary nearby, but it is on an Army Base. It's just not the same. Also, I have friends in the Hampton Roads area I have not seen in a few years, and I get to visit one of my old stomping grounds...Naval Amphibious Base Chief Petty Officer's Club. It will be good to breathe sailor air and reminisce about the 'good ole days'. Good night my friend.

Chapter 10

Monday, September 20, 1999

"Welcome aboard..."

*T*he last time I boarded a naval vessel was 1995. Even though it's only been four years I am still feeling just a tad bit intimidated. As I stand here on the pier, ready to board the USS GREENWOOD LAKE (AD-30), with my head bent all the way back so that I can see the whole ship, all I could think about is how glad I am I decided to wear a pants suit and very comfortable shoes!

The ship's Legal Officer, Lieutenant Zachariah Wilson, who will be one of my escorts for the next couple days, met me on the quarterdeck. "Welcome aboard Dr. Morgan. Thank you so much for taking time to come aboard." *He seemed friendly towards me knowing I'm the investigator that will probably make his job harder than what it already is.*

Lieutenant Wilson gave me a tour of the ship, introduced me to crewmembers passing by, the Administrative Officer,

Lieutenant Sonja Alejandro and a few others he thought would be assisting me during my investigation. The Captain was not onboard at the time, but he introduced me to other officers and enlisted personnel. They were all polite. I thought it was strange he did not introduce me to the command master chief, especially since I made sure he knew I was retired chief petty officer. I even requested a space to work in or near the Chief's Mess so that I would be closer to the sailors I would be interviewing. Lieutenant Wilson said the Captain thought I would be more "comfortable" near the Wardroom. I was given an office that I expect was a closet until yesterday. I'm sure there is a story.

The morning was spent with Lieutenant Wilson giving me a quick tour and introducing me to this crewmember and that crewmember. The tour ended in the wardroom for lunch with the Commanding Officer, Captain John Greyson. Again, I still have not met the Command Master Chief, BMCM(SW) Jonathan Hudson. No one mentioned that he was not onboard the ship, so why wasn't he available.

I did not start preparing for interviews until after lunch. By about two o'clock I could not handle breathing my own carbon monoxide in the closet office they put me in. I called

Lieutenant Wilson to take me to meet Master Chief Hudson. He obliged me, but I could tell he was hesitant. Interesting.

Master Chief Hudson gave me permission to hangout in the Chief's Mess whenever I wanted. When I told him where the office was they gave me, he was kind enough to find me a space that was much more suitable and more convenient for interviews.

"Dr. Morgan you have been away for a little while, but I'm sure shipboard dynamics have not changed that much. This case, involving Jackson, his request and Harvey makes the dynamics much more extreme."

"Why is that?"

"Although I don't have proof, I think someone wants us to believe the disappearance of Jackson's officer package occurred because Harvey is trying to hinder his progress and possible promotion, thus the feud between the two of them."

"And you don't feel that is correct?"

"No, I don't. I believe this entire situation is being orchestrated by someone hiding something that either Jackson or Harvey has witnessed or have information about. Also, the fear of you opening the closet full of skeletons the rest of us don't know about is a problem. So, the hope was you would not show up at all, and now that you have, the intent is to whisk you away as quickly as possible."

"Starting with the closet office," *I interjected.*

He laughed, "Yes, the closet office."

"Doc…may I call you Doc? It may be a little bit too informal for you."

"I would prefer you call me Doc in here," *smiling, nodding towards the entrance to the Chief's Mess,* "but not out there. It will be important to make sure everyone understand who has the last word."

"Including me, I'm sure", said Master Chief Hudson. "And you may call me Jonathan in here, but not out there", as he nodded towards the entrance.

They both laughed. "Doc, I just want to assure you that you have the support of the crew to help you with your investigation. I have had both Jackson and Harvey in my office concerning the harassment charges and Jackson's request.

While we were chatting, the ship's counselor, NCC(SW) Elizabeth Franklin walked in talking before she saw me. "The madness is real out there. Oh, hello Dr. Morgan (*as she looked first at me, then Jonathan, then me again*), "It's good to meet you. They call me Beth in here." *Shaking her hand,* "It's good to meet you too."

As she walked over to get coffee, "I was not on board this morning otherwise I would have greeted you instead of Lieutenant Wilson. I'm sure he was shaking in his boots." *Her laugh was full and hardy as if she's the one breathing life into wherever she is.* "I have been waiting to meet you, along with other female ship's counselors in Hampton Roads. I bet you didn't know you are famous, did you?"

"Um, famous…me…why would I be famous?"

"Come on now, I know you know that you are one of the pioneers of female ship's counselors in the Navy and THE pioneer in this area! I know you know this. There were no other female ship's counselors here before you. You were the first!"

"No, I don't think I was the first female ship's counselor in Hampton Roads. I was the first female base counselor but not onboard a ship."

"Yes you were. I did the research. You were both. How could you not have known that!?"

"I guess I never paid it much attention at the time. I was so busy I didn't have time to realize I was "famous," especially on my ship which decommissioned a year after I came aboard. That was a nightmare!"

Chief Franklin replied, shaking her head, "And now you are here, back in the madness again. I hope we have time to talk about your experiences before you leave."

"I'm sure we will", *replied Dr. Morgan.* "I'm going to meet some of my old friends, who retired in the area, at the Chief's Club at the Naval Amphibious Base. You are welcome to come along if you like. I'm sure the stories will be interesting, to say the least. This "new" Navy is a sight to behold (shaking my head and frowning). I don't have anything planned for tomorrow evening after I leave here. I plan to do most of my work Tuesday and Wednesday, so I'm not sure how long I will be on board each night. I'll be flying Friday afternoon back to Atlanta."

Chief Franklin sighed, "Well, hopefully we will find time. I've already notified everyone you will be interviewing and made sure they knew what time they needed to be in your office. I have also left room for impromptu meetings. I will make sure you have your copy of the schedule before you leave today. A yeoman and I will be available to take care of any administrative work you will need. Just let me know."

"Okay, thank you very much. I'll be here another hour or so. Thanks to the Master Chief I have a decent office to work out of."

Sitting in my very comfortable office, as shipboard offices go, I'm working through a hodgepodge of information received from the ship and Commander Scott. I have a copy of Petty Officer Jackson's request for the officer's program he is applying for. I have pre-recorded statements from crewmembers saying Petty Officer Harvey "had it out" for Jackson, or vice versa, from the beginning. I will be speaking to these crewmembers myself. The more I look at this pile of paper, the more I sense what I need is not here. I have my work cut out for me and very little time to do it in.

Lieutenant Wilson bought me more paperwork from his office. Some I had, some I didn't. Oddly enough, the original copy of Petty Officer Jackson's officer candidate package was not in the stack. When I asked about it he said it was never given to him. As he and I talked, I continued to feel something was being held back, either by him or from him. To be honest,

I expect it's the latter. I reminded him of the importance of getting ALL of the facts on the table so the matter can be settled fairly and swiftly. He nodded as if he agreed, but the look in his eyes told me he knew that was not going to happen.

Chief Franklin came by to bring me the schedule. "Don't be too hard on Lieutenant Wilson. He's a pawn on a very shaky chess board waiting for his turn to be kicked off the board as soon as something or someone better comes along. Don't get me wrong, I think he's a very good lawyer who lost his confidence somewhere along the way. Also, although he is the legal officer, he really has little say about anything on this ship. He just kinda does what he's told. He told me he has a friend in the base legal office that helps him with cases, especially this one. I will tell you Natalee, this case is a mess."

"Why do you say that?" *I remember Scotty mentioning the legal officer. I did not know they were "friends". Hmmm.*

She got up and closed the door, "Just think about it. First there is the rivalry. They are polar opposites. Harvey came here with a less than stella reputation. I spoke to his last ship's counselor and the story is not pretty. He was not promotion-to-chief worthy then and he has not done much to improve his worthiness. He had not blatantly done anything to warrant demotion or separation, until recently. His evals are average, just enough. Everything about him is just enough. There were always several first-class petty officers in his division on his previous ships so it was never a concern about him becoming a leading petty officer. Here, it is a different story. The leading petty officer in his division is transferring shortly and Harvey is the only first-class petty officer for now. Harvey could automatically become the leading petty officer by default."

"Excuse me for interrupting you. You said 'until recently' when you were saying that Harvey had not gotten into any trouble. What changed?"

"Harvey accused Jackson of improperly completing and submitting a report concerning a test they were conducting in the engine room while we were underway. Everyone knew Jackson did the test correctly and completed the proper report, but Harvey insisted he did not. So, an investigation was initiated. The results proved Harvey to be wrong. He got angry, which he does a lot, and accused Senior Chief Patrick and Commander Matson of favoring their 'Golden blank-

blank Boy" over him. Harvey goes to disciplinary review board next week."

"Dr. Morgan, I am not a psychologist like you, however, I think he lost it because he is jealous of Jackson and he assumes everyone is out to get him. I think he is also worried if Jackson took the exam and passed it would cause problems for him. So, he accused Jackson of this wrongdoing a week before the exams, in the hope that he would be denied an opportunity to test until after the investigation was completed. I guess Harvey thought it would seal his assignment to leading petty officer. Since there was proof Jackson did nothing wrong, the command allowed him to take the exam while the investigation was going on."

"You all were that sure Jackson was innocent?"

"Sure enough, and worst-case scenario, if he passed the exam high enough to be advanced, the command could revoke his advancement if he was guilty. This is Jackson's first attempt at taking the exam, so his results could go either way. (*She shook her head*) However, I think Harvey was, and still is, worried his promotion to leading petty officer would be in jeopardy if Jackson passes the exam. We will find out next week when the exam results are posted.

"Beth, what makes him so worried that Jackson would be promoted? Why would he have jeopardized what little he has on a maybe? I would never attempt to diagnose him, however, if I were to give a name to how you all are saying he acts, it would be Borderline Personality Disorder."

"What is that?"

"It's when people cause problems in their surroundings in order to divert what they presume to be a problem pointing to them."

"Oh. Well remember I said they were polar opposites. I meant that literally. Petty Officer Jackson is the Straight A student in the engineering department. He came into the Navy with an associate's degree in mechanical engineering. He aced every Navy school he has attended. He is very smart. Sometimes, too smart. His peers and supervisors love him and at the same time plot to throw him overboard the next time we are underway. He has teed off several shipmates because he "politely" corrected them concerning one thing or another. And when I say politely, I mean po-lite-ly! He is a very spiritual man. He does not curse and very seldom yells. He said his parents taught him how to communicate without cursing. Most of the time his demeanor was pretty mellow.

He is one of those 'don't take my kindness for weakness' kinda guys. One or two learned that lesson the hard way, including Harvey. He was never disrespectful, just direct and to the point."

"The letter we received indicates Petty Officer Jackson was being harassed because of his religion and because he asked to become an officer. Has his being a Sabbath-keeper caused contention between him and his peers and or supervisors. How does this effect the way he and Petty Officer Harvey get along?"

"I heard about the letter but had no reason to get involved in my capacity as Ship's Counselor. I also am not involved with daily work rotations in the departments. I have heard of instances where he has asked to trade a Saturday for a Sunday, which were granted. I heard of an incident where Petty Officer Harvey disapproved a request because he said he needed Jackson onboard that one Saturday. The request was initiated by another crew member who needed Sunday off and was approved the rest of the way up the chain."

Nodding my head, "I have investigated similar cases concerning religion and the workplace. There is always a common denominator that pulls all of the complaints together…the religion in question is different than the norm and the complainer is always unwilling to compromise. Based on what he and others have said, Harvey is not religious, which means this case has nothing to do with religion."

Beth did not respond but looked as if she was contemplating if her thoughts should be shared now or later.

After an acceptable length of silence I said, "Well Beth, we have a very intense and very long couple of days ahead of us. I'm headed to meet friends and then to the lodge for some rest. I'll see you in the morning."

"Natalee, what time do you plan to be onboard in the morning? Your first appointment is not until 9:30."

"I plan to be here about eight o'clock. I left my breakfast request with my young chef, which I'm sure will be much more appealing than coffee, boiled eggs and a dry danish at the hotel."

They both laughed. "Beth have a good evening if I don't see you at The Club."

As I stepped on the pier, I turned to look at the ship and asked her, "What are you hiding from me…"

September 20, 1999

10:30 p.m.

Dear Diary. Today was a good day and a very tiring day. I went aboard a naval vessel today for the first time since I retired. It felt a little bit weird and invigorating all at the same time. I got plenty of exercise walking up and down and all around that ship today. No need to look for the hotel treadmill.

As ship's dynamics and personalities go, not much has changed in four years. There are many secrets and I have a feeling several of them surround what's going on with Petty Officers Jackson and Harvey. I'll figure it out tomorrow.

This evening I had a wonderful time with friends at the Chief's Club. I know I had missed hanging out with sailors, but I didn't know how much I missed it until today. Ha! Ha! Not enough to want to move back here though. It is September and it is already COLD up here. I did not pack for cold weather. I had to go to the Exchange and buy sweaters and a jacket so that I can dress in layers. Who knows what the weather will be like tomorrow. There is no way I'd move back here. Nancy said it is 70 degrees at home.

I did talk to Tracy this evening. I will be happy to see him when I return. We don't have much time left. I want to enjoy him as much as I can before he leaves forever.

Well, I need to rest. I have a feeling tomorrow will be nerve-racking to say the least. The GREENWOOD LAKE is full of secrets and closets with skeletons trying to get out. Hopefully, I will open a few closets tomorrow. Good night.

Chapter 11

Tuesday, September 21, 1999

"Sometimes a big head..."

*B*reakfast in the Chief's Mess. Another perk I had pushed to the back of my brain. Yesterday a very crisp young seaman came to my office to ask me what I wanted for breakfast, lunch and dinner. She gave me three menus and said she would return in about 30 minutes to get my selection. I was swooning for a moment. I had forgotten what it was like to have someone treat me so wonderfully. Yes, it was her job, but she was on her job.

I decided to use my time during breakfast to get more information about the sailors involved in this case. Once again, the descriptions were similar to Beth's. Day and night, or oil and water, or Peter Pan and Captain Hook. I had to laugh, because without asking about the actual harassment case, again I could tell the real case is not about religious discrimination but something much deeper and more sinister than which day someone prefers to worship.

After breakfast I sat in my office reviewing my schedule for the day. I pulled out the interview schedule Chief Franklin had created for me. I like her. Thorough. The list was actually a folder with a separate sheet for each interview. At the top of the sheet is Name/Division/Date/Time of Interview. The next section was a quick biography of the interviewee. The rest of the sheet was for my notes. I smiled. I would hire her.

Five minutes before the first interviewee was to arrive the telephone rings.

"Hello, Dr. Morgan speaking…"

"Hello, Dr. Morgan, how are you doing?"

I'm sure my outside face showed how excited I was not to hear his voice. "Commander Scott, I'm fine, how are you?" *I wondered how long it would take for him to call. I'm not in the mood this early in the morning.*

"I was surprised when Zach told me you were in town. Why didn't you call to let me know you were coming?"

"Commander why would I have called you?"

"I thought we were going to be partners on this case. I was surprised to learn that you are onboard the GREENWOOD LAKE. I hope they are treating you well."

"Actually, yes they are. Thank you for your concern. I have to go—"

As is his habit and with an unmistakable attitude, Commander Scott interrupts me...

"After our meeting in Atlanta I thought we were on the same page concerning this case, I didn't expect you to come to Norfolk. I am a little bewildered as to why you felt it necessary and without contacting me first! Now that you are here we can finally have that dinner and catch up..."

At this point I am unable to maintain a peaceful attitude, and so I interrupted him...

"Commander Scott, if you will remember, I told you I would be doing my due diligence for the case before I make a decision concerning the final outcome. Also, if you will recall, there were no decisions made in Atlanta because there were no questions answered. So, I'm not really sure what you mean by 'on the same page' and that I should have contacted you first."

"I brought you the documents of my investigation and my recommendations. What else do you need to be satisfied that the ship is not at fault here?" "I'm just saying...

I wanted to ask him at fault about what, but I didn't want the conversation to continue.

"Commander Scott I fear you have taken my tolerance as an invitation for you to continue to interfere with my investigation. Because of my concern for the enlisted men and women on this ship, I am saying this as politely as I can under the circumstances. I have work to do here and I have a crewmember that was taken away from his duties and is waiting to speak to me. You know the protocol for congressional investigations, and you know you were out of order when you came to Atlanta unannounced and uninvited. I will not have this conversation with you. I will reach out to you IF I need your assistance. Also, might I remind you I have the last word concerning the life of this case, not you. Thank you and have a nice day."

My bad angel: "Girl you told him...GOOD JOB!"

My good angel: "I have to agree with her. I was praying for me and you!"

What is he trying to hide.

Chapter 12

"sometimes a threat is a promise..."

"Dr..., hello, **HELLO!**"

*C*ommander Scott literally slams the phone on the receiver and starts a slow, somewhat loud, string of obscenities as he storms out of his office.

"How dare she hang up on me. Who does she think she is? Does she know who I am? She is just a glorified records keeper. No one talks to me like that...and then hangs up! What makes her think she is in charge of anything! I am in charge of this situation, not her!" *More obscenities.*

By the time he walked from his office to his car he was a little bit calm, but not really. He could not wrap his head around the fact that Nattie hung up on him. His Nattie, who use to be a little timid records keeper in the Navy.

Talking almost out loud, "I don't know what her record of cases won is, but she needs to know that I have never lost a real case. Yes,

I was a little off my game when I saw her, but I had no doubt I had convinced them there was no case when I was in Atlanta. I just can't figure out why she rushed to...ahhh (smiling big as if it had all come clear) she must want to get with me after all! HA!HA! But why the phone hang-up. She knows my job is to protect the Navy and she is trying to be a defense lawyer. She is out of her league and playing hard. I'll have to just cool her down a little bit.

Now that he has calmed down a little bit, Scotty is devising a plan to woo the good doctor right out of her...case. That country sheriff of hers won't know what happened.

As he walked back into the office, he is formulating a plan. Without breaking his stride he says to his assistant, "Call Lieutenant Wilson onboard the GREENWOOD LAKE. Let him know I will be onboard tomorrow at 10:00."

"Sir, he's in your office."

"What?!"

"Lieutenant Wilson came in right after you stormed...I mean, stepped out. He is waiting in your office. He seems a little frazzled."

Commander Scott responded with a frown, "Thank you."

Lieutenant Wilson paced the floor looking at this accolade or that accolade heralding Commander Scott's accomplishments throughout his career.

He murmured to himself, "Well, Scotty, old boy, this case will not be an attribute to your brilliance..."

"Say what Zach. I heard you talking to yourself, again. What's up with that", *Scotty laughed,* "What brings you here? How is the investigation going?"

"It's not!", *Lieutenant Wilson muttered as he sat down,* "I've only known her one day and I know she is going to figure everything out and then where is that going to leave me. I came to you with a real issue and you turned it into something altogether different. She's asking questions I don't have the answers to." *Zachariah is pacing the floor again, voice elevating,* "People may try to treat me as if my name is "Boo-Boo-the-Fool", but I am not risking my career over some petty issues between..."

"Lower you voice, what is wrong with you!" *Scotty almost shouted,* "Any louder and everything you say will be in the next edition of Stars and Stripes! What is going on over there. I called her and she basically hung up on me!"

"Basically? How does someone basically hang up on you Scotty? In other words, she didn't succumb to your charms. It's obvious whatever you all had, is just that…HAD! Now, how are you going to fix this mess. She is turning stones and opening closets, and skeletons are falling out. She meets with Commander Miller in the morning, who is already looking at me one-eyed, and depending on that conversation, my head will be on a platter, not yours! So, what are YOU going to do about HER, because I'm telling you now, I will not be walking the plank alone!"

Commander Scott stood from his chair, "Are you trying to give me some kind of ultimatum, Lieutenant Wilson?"

"No Sir, Commander Scott. I don't know what you have going on, with whomever you have it going on with on that ship, and I don't want to know. What I do know is that I will not be the fall guy when Commander Miller summons me in her 'WHAT THE…' voice! She will want answers that I don't have. But you know what I do have…names, dates, places and things, and I will be giving her all of them.

Lieutenant Wilson stood and walked to the door, "That sir, is a promise!"

Chapter 13

"When your Spirit hurts"

O nce I finally looked at my watch it was 1215. I had interviewed five crewmembers, including Petty Officer Jackson. My young seaman calls to let me know my lunch would be ready in 15 minutes. So I called Chief Franklin and met her for lunch. It was delicious. I got to meet more Chiefs. One of which was the Engineering Chief, ENSC(SW) Patricia Anthony. She is Harvey and Jackson's lead supervisor.

"Dr. Morgan, I'm sure you have already heard my two Petty Officers are as different as day and night. Jackson is very people oriented. Harvey is not. Jackson is very confident in himself and his abilities, which sometimes gets him in trouble, but all the time puts him in a position to help the rest of his shipmates. Harvey does not."

"There is more to Harvey than what we see on the surface. Something happened, who knows how long ago, before he came here. He is angry all the time and seems to be in a dark secluded place the majority of the time.

She told me a story that happened last year which helped me to understand why she felt Harvey was in a dark place.

"It was the policy of the ship to submit request for holiday leave in advance. They were allowed to choose the week of Christmas or the week of New Year's. The deadline for submitting their leave requests was November 1st. Everyone in the department submitted their request for holiday leave early, everyone except EN1 Harvey. At that point, he had been onboard almost a year, and I know he did not take leave when he transferred to us. I was told by the personnelman Harvey was in jeopardy of losing some of his leave because he had too many days on the books. When I asked why he had not taken leave or submitted a request for holiday leave, his response was he had no place to go for the holidays so why waste his time. Besides if everyone else is out gallivanting around the world for the holidays who would do the work. He was adamant he did not want to "gallivant." I could tell he was angry about everyone else who submitted a request so they could gallivant, as he put it, through the holidays. He especially made a point to complain that EN2 Jackson had also submitted a request to take off during the

Thanksgiving holiday. He said, "nobody needs to be around his family that much."

"Harvey said asking for leave insinuated he had someone looking forward to seeing him...and he didn't. Both his parents were dead and he and his siblings get along from afar. They show up for required appearances like funerals. And since both their parents were dead there would be very little reason to do much connecting. They were good with a phone call every now and again. He and his ex-wife have been divorced for about five years. Despite the bad blood between him and his ex-wife, he does have an amicable relationship with his tween children, especially if he has gifts for them and sends money when they ask for it. So, it's easier to just send money and make a call every now and then."

"Eventually I was successful in convincing him to at least take a few days off so he did not lose leave days. He decided to take a few days to visit with his children over the Christmas break. When he returned from visiting his family I asked him about his time with his daughters. He looked at me with his 'why-do-you-care' look on his face and said it was okay. Everyone was showing pictures and talking about their trip, except him.

As far as I know he has no friends on this ship. I think the only person that he talks to is the personnelman, PN1 Deloris Richards.

After an extended pause Patricia continued, "I don't know why anyone would think that Jackson is being discriminated against. The people in his chain of command think very highly of him. We have all types of religions or no religion on the ship. Everyone does their job. You may have heard about the time Harvey recommended disapproval of a request for Jackson to switch with someone. He was the section leader that day. It was actually comical because he was so pleased with himself. The request was approved anyway. And I know you know about the pending disciplinary review board for Harvey. I don't know what he was thinking. However, as impulsive as he is, I'm still finding it hard to believe that Harvey had anything to do with the disappearance of Jackson's package."

"Why?"

Patricia continued, "Because Harvey does not have access to Jackson's service record or officer's package."

Natalee responded, "But PN1 Richards does."

Both Chiefs looked at me raised eyebrows and responded at the same time, "What are you saying!"

"Patricia, did you sign Jackson's request?"

"Yes!"

"Did you recommend approval or disapproval?"

"I was the one that initiated the request and the package. I discussed it with Commander Mattson, and Master Chief Hudson. They both agreed Jackson was more than qualified for the program. Everyone in Jackson's immediate chain of command recommended approval of the request and forwarded the package. Harvey is not in Jackson's chain of command, so he had no say in the matter. I made a copy with all of our signatures on it."

Natalee asked, "Who did the package go to after you all signed it?"

"Normally I would have given it to Beth. I didn't this time because Commander Mattson was headed in that direction for a department head meeting so he said he would give it to her."

"Beth...?"

Beth responded, "He gave it to me at the department head meeting, I made sure the appropriate boxes were checked, and gave it to Lieutenant Alejandro, at the same meeting. However, I remember getting it back from her later that day before it was forwarded to the executive officer because I forgot to make my copy. That's why the copy you have has her signature on it. I thought it was strange she still had it instead of leaving it with the executive officer, but I didn't dwell on it...until now."

"Then what happened to it?"

"Dr. Morgan where exactly are you going with this. I feel like I'm in an interrogation of some sort," *said Beth. Patricia nodded in agreement.*

"I was sent here to investigate two complaints for religious discrimination and harassment. The religious discrimination case is obviously not true. However, the accusation that someone on this ship is preventing Petty Officer Jackson his right to submit a package for a program he is clearly eligible for is still an issue. Why is that? Everyone is saying they don't know what happened to the package. Since the last place you all know it was seen was with the Admin Officer, whose desk is in the personnel office, it is probable that that's where it was last seen. Otherwise, Commander Miller or Captain Grayson has it. If they are in favor of Jackson applying for the program, why would one, or both of them conceal it? What's Lieutenant Alejandro's story?"

"Wait, explain that look and the shaking of the heads. What is that all about?"

Beth responded, "Normally, I would have made a copy of the entire package, but I decided to wait until Captain Grayson signed it. When I gave the package to Lieutenant Alejandro it was intact. When I found out Commander Miller did not have it, I went to get it from Lieutenant Alejandro to get the signatures myself. Lieutenant Alejandro said she left instructions for it to be delivered to Commander Miller, so, she no longer had it. It struck me as very strange that she didn't know where it was. The next day I asked her again, same response. So I decided not to worry about the original package until I remembered there were attachments to the package that would take too long to reproduce, especially since the deadline for submission is in two weeks, and, we are preparing to get underway in a week. Then Lieutenant Alejandro told me, very nonchalantly, that only the original package with original signatures and attachments could be mailed in. How did she know that and I didn't?"

"Natalee, any suspicions you have are probably accurate and lead to the personnel office. However, the problem is, there are still too many puzzle pieces that don't fit anywhere. I have asked everyone working in the personnel office several times what happened to the package after she signed it. The explanation is always shady... "I'll get back to you..." or "You haven't found it yet?" In my kindest voice I could muster I reminded her that I did not lose it."

"I have been on the verge of locking everyone in the office until they pull it from under wherever it is hiding!", *Beth said, a little irritation in her voice.*

"So now what?" *asked Patricia.*

"So, tell me her story? How does she fit? As I've already said, this investigation has nothing to do with religion and more to do with someone not wanting Jackson to be selected for this program. The deadline is coming up and the package cannot be forwarded without Captain Grayson's approval. Also, what does all of this to do with the feud between Harvey and Jackson? Is Harvey really the hateful, prejudice-looking person he is portrayed to be, or, is someone else fueling the fire between Harvey and Jackson in order to cover up something else…and what would that be?"

Silently Natalee also wonders where Commander Scott and Lieutenant Wilson fit in all of this.

Patricia said with a quickness, "I can tell you this, Lieutenant Alejandro is one angry sister, but if you want to talk about her, we need to do it someplace else, not here!"

Chapter 14

Wednesday, September 22, 1999

"Big Ears...Small Morals"

"...rid yourselves of all malice and all deceit..."

(1 Peter 2:1a)

*L*ieutenant Sonja Alejandro is first generation American born Hispanic. Her grandparents migrated to America from Cuba in 1955. A glitch in the system allowed her grandfather to come to America on a permanent work visa with his family. Her father was ten years old at the time, and as soon as he graduated from high school he joined the Navy. Since it was the beginning of the Vietnam War he was able to join the Navy without becoming an American citizen. He was also promised citizenship if he remained on active duty for a certain amount of time. He didn't know if that was true or not, but he was happy to join the Navy instead of being drafted into the Army like most of his graduating classmates. After his first tour of duty he married his high school sweetheart Madalyne. Madalyne graduated from college as a nurse.

They had five children, of which Sonja is next to the youngest and the only girl. Her father and two of her brothers are career Sailors. One of her brother's wanted nothing to do with Vietnam or it's issues. He decided it was his job to make sure his family and friends did not allow the government to rob them blind, so he became an accountant and a personal finance counselor. Her youngest brother planned to become a professional soccer player. Because she spent all of her four years of high school in the Navy Reserve Officers Training Corp, Sonja chose the Navy because she received a full four-year scholarship and officer commission upon successful completion of college and Officer Candidate School.

The family competition continues since she is the first female in her family to join the military, and the first officer. Although she came into the Navy because that's what she always wanted to do, she felt she really had something to prove to her father and brothers, as well as to the world...that she was more than "just a woman" and that she was just as good as the men in her family and in the world.

The USS GREENWOOD LAKE is Lieutenant Alejandro's second duty station after completing Officer Candidate School. Her first position as a naval officer was as the Administrative Officer for Norfolk Naval Station, Norfolk Virginia. It was the type of job that touched all of her senses. It was fulfilling and nerve-racking. She worked for two commanders that were as different as full moon and no moon. Her first commander had gotten used to working with women, but she was his first female officer working directly in his inner circle. He made both of them miserable. As time went on she learned his personalities and was able to work a full day without vowing to put several drops of Saint John's Wart in his coffee. She took solace in realizing she was not the only one that prayed he would transfer tomorrow. Some of them wanted to put something much more dangerous and possibly illegal in his coffee.

Eventually he left and the new Commander was much more "chilled," if you can say such a thing when describing a base commander. Her working life became much more tolerable, and she was able to really enjoy her job and all of the people she worked with. Whenever possible he would send her and a couple of the other women, both officer and enlisted, on short deployments aboard ships so they would become familiar with shipboard work and living. Of course it was always for official duty, but she appreciated the confidence he had in her as a sailor and as an administrator. He also encouraged her to learn everything there is to know about being the education officer because, most of the time, the education and administration officers are the same person. The first thing she was told upon choosing the GREENWOOD LAKE was she would be both.

About six months after Sonja arrived onboard the GREENWOOD LAKE, the ship received a new commanding officer. She could not believe her luck. Most people go through their entire career without serving with the same people. How is it that he was her first and now third commanding officer. "What did I do to you God," she thought. Within the first couple of months of him arriving, she realized he had not changed, and in some instances, he was worse.

Captain John Grayson preferred the "Old Navy" where women were barely in the Navy. When he joined, women were only "allowed" in certain non-combatant positions and definitely not allowed on any ships, except maybe hospital ships as medical staff. After leaving shore duty he prayed for a peaceful sea tour free of women. Unfortunately, his wishes were not granted. His ship was selected to receive the first female crewmembers ordered to this class of ship. His wife, warned him many times to "get with the program." But he refused. Now it's too late, and as a result, he will not be promoted to Admiral, He will be forced to retired in a couple years. It wasn't that he didn't like women, but as far as he was concerned, they had their place…in a house taking care of children and making sure dinner is ready. Not in the Navy, and definitely not onboard ships. On his last ship most of the officers were men. As much as possible, he ignored the two female officers assigned to his ship. Now, on the GREENWOOD LAKE, he is forced to contend with women in several positions he could not ignore, including the executive officer. So, he is a mean, cranky curmudgeon the majority of the time.

Sonja could not understand how one person could hold on to hatred like that and live. In her position as the administrative and education officer she had to work directly with both the executive officer and commanding officer. Most days he tried to crush her spirit, but she held her head high as much as possible. And she bided her time because she is no longer that young naïve ensign he tortured back then. Her day will come when she will crush his spirit.

A few months after he arrived, she "discovered" he was not eligible for promotion and GREENWOOD LAKE would be his last command. Further "investigation" led her to learn his inability to be promoted stemmed from a messy discrimination and harassment case. She also found out that EN1 Harvey came from that same ship. She wondered if EN2 Jackson was involved somehow which might explain the feud between the two petty officers. She did not know who else onboard was privy to this "valuable" information, but she deduced that it would become useful in the future. She did, however, decide to talk to her boyfriend to see if he would be able to help her if she needed him.

EN1 Harvey was not very popular on the ship and only had one or two "friends" onboard. One of his friends was the lead

Personalman, PN1 Richards. It turned out that they had a few things in common. Richards was raised in Clayton, Mississippi, which was only 15 miles from Harvey's hometown of Natchez, Mississippi. Also, they were both divorced and like Harvey, Richards was also in jeopardy of not being promoted. It was overheard, on more than one occasion, Harvey voicing his dislike for Jackson, complaining about his accomplishment, military and personal, and how he is always flaunting his knowledge and his stuff, while quoting scripture. He said Jackson reminded him of those hypocrite television preachers, always pretending they talk directly to Jesus while they are robbing people blind. Because Jackson never seemed to be broke and he drove a nice car, Harvey continually insinuated Jackson must be a part-time drug dealer or something, because there is no way he could afford the things he had with the salary he made.

Harvey was overheard telling Richards if he were the leading petty officer he would take joy in knocking Jackson down a peg or two and putting him in his place. It is always said that if you are going to verbally relay what is floating around in your head... make sure your words can't come back to bite you one day.

Unfortunately for EN1 Harvey, Lieutenant Alejandro, just happen to be the one within ear shot of this particular conversation and she knew exactly how to use it and EN1 Harvey to make what *she needed to happen, happen. Of course, when the time came, she knew just the person to call to make it all legal.*

Chapter 15

Wednesday, September 22, 1999

Deceit and Lies

"A false witness will not go unpunished..." (Proverbs 19:9a)

E N1 Harvey walked out of his second conversation with Dr. Morgan. He went to the First Class Lounge for a drink. Unfortunately, he would not find beer there. Black coffee would have to do. He was sick and tired of everyone asking him if he knew anything about Jackson's missing package for that stupid officer program. He did not have the package, but he almost told Dr. Morgan he knew what happened to it...until he remembered the threat. If he cooperated, he was told his disciplinary review board situation would go away, and he would get the leading petty officer position. If he did not cooperate, he would end up in Fort Leavenworth for a couple years on multiple charges of falsifying government documents and harassment, along with a bad conduct discharge instead of retirement. If he had known...he would never have accepted orders to this ship...there were three other ships he could have chosen. All he wanted to do was be advanced to chief before he retired. If that was not possible, he just wanted to get out of Dodge without going to prison. However, the minute he saw 'him' he knew two things. First, this ship was going to be the same hell as his last; and second, if he didn't play his cards right, he could end up in prison with no advancement and no retirement.

Harvey felt from birth he was doomed to be trouble or get into trouble. That's what his parents always told him. He was told he was lazy and would never amount to much, even when he was doing good…it was never enough. When he joined the Navy he thought that stigma would go away. It didn't. Even when he wasn't being lazy or amounting to nothing, just like at home, he always seemed to be accused for what he did and what they did…whomever 'they' happened to be at the time.

One of his biggest shortfalls, in the Navy and in life, is his very low perception of the usefulness of women and where their place in life fell. Of all the horrible traits of his father he could have pattern behind, he chose this one.

Women were in the Navy before he joined and they would be after he left. He tolerated them on shore duty. He figured they really weren't intruding on his territory because he did not have to work with women who were enginemen or mechanics of any kind, mainly because most of the time he was not working as an engineman *himself. His superiors always seemed to find jobs for him to do outside of his assigned department and a woman always seemed to take his place. He just assumed that everyone was out to get him, including women.*

Shortly after reporting to his last ship he realized that women were going to be assigned, some of which would be in the engineering department and in his division. He was furious! He prided himself on making a point of not accepting orders to ships with women on them. Although he was not the lead supervisor of the division, he was responsible for work and duty schedules which allowed him many occasions to harass them, and he took advantage of all of them. He was going to teach them and the Navy that women did not belong on ships.

On several occasions, there were accusations of harassment towards women on the ship, most of which could not be proven. Eventually, he went too far and was put on report with sufficient evidence supporting the accusations against him. The report stated he consistently adjusted the work schedule so the women were put on jobs no one else wanted. At one point he assigned a woman a task she was not qualified to perform and then reprimanded her for not completing the task correctly.

This incident became a very serious charge of gender discrimination. The disciplinary review board recommended reduction in rate. However, when the case was placed before the commanding officer it was dismissed with no explanation, no repercussions for Harvey. Instead of an apology to the woman involved, she was reassigned, without explanation. She filed a discrimination accusation against the ship. Her case was filed inconclusive and everyone carried on with their lives. Everyone, except EN1 Harvey.

Although the accusation were dismissed, his assignment as the scheduling petty officer was given to a younger member of the division. To his dismay, a younger member was now assigning him duties, some of which were jobs he'd previously pawned off to women. EN1 Harvey's life became unbearable, not only at work, but personally as well. His misfortunes were everyone else's fault.

He continued his career working towards retirement, however, that year, he was not allowed to test for advancement. In the dark corners of his mind he knew on paper he would never be eligible for promotion. He was angry. He wanted to blame everyone…to say everyone had it out for him. However, he knew better, and he knew he would have to do something before they find a reason to demote him before he retires.

When he finally transferred from the ship he thought he would start over and at least have one more opportunity for promotion before his retirement. When he walked onboard he realized his worst

116

nightmare. On the quarterdeck were pictures of the four most important people on the ship. He could not believe his eyes. How could this be happening to him. Whatever is below hell...he just arrived.

So it's not all about Jackson. It was easy enough to dislike Jackson. Even before Harvey transferred to the ship he heard about him. Another young sailor who thought he was better. Jackson is some kind of engineman guru, which is why everyone thinks he would make a great officer? Harvey would rather slit his own throat than to work for Jackson, in any capacity. However, none of them are worth his retirement. So, he will keep his mouth shut for a little while longer, as long as his retirement is not in jeopardy. If his retirement is threatened, he will squeal like some of those pigs whose throats he slit back on the farm.

As he gulped the last of his now cold coffee, he smiled and thought, "I will not be the scape-goat this time, and, I am not going to prison...but I do know who will...I know who will." *While he was still smiling a flash shot across his mind made him remember a scripture from Sunday School when he was a child, "Even fools are thought wise if they keep silent, and discerning if they hold their tongues" (Proverbs 17:28). He had not been to church or broke the seal on a Bible in years, so he had to wonder where that thought came from and why. Then he smiled, but it's good advice…good advice.*

Chapter 16

"Hell has no fury like a cornered lawyer"

*I*t was 4:00 p.m. and Commander Scott was still fuming about the conversation with Dr. Morgan and then with Lieutenant Wilson. As a result of his foul disposition, the three court cases he had after his conversations with Dr. Morgan and Lieutenant Wilson suffered severely. In all three cases he argued with the defense lawyer, the defendant, the witnesses and even the judge. He lost one case when the judge dismissed it because of his conduct. Now his tantrums are seriously out of control. He had not lost a case in YEARS! Of course he blamed Lieutenant Wilson and Dr. Morgan for his mishaps. He could not believe either of them spoke to him the way they did. They obviously don't know who they are dealing with, especially, Lieutenant Wilson. "I could have him shipped to Never-Never Land with the *(as he snapped his fingers)* SNAP of my fingers!"

As for Nattie, I guess she thinks she is out of my reach. I will have her eating out of my hand soon enough. Just as he was about to

leave his office, his cell phone rang. The minute he looked at the
number he cursed.

"Hello Sir, how are you doing?"

"No Sir I don't have a handle on her...yet."

"I thought so too, but obviously I was mistaken. It's not that simple."

"Sir, I will handle her!"

He snatches the phone away from his ear as he hears the caller
cussing and then slamming the phone down.

Scotty yells a few choice words of his own as he puts his phone in
his pocket, "I'm done." *And then a thought came to his head. He*
smiled as he retrieved his phone and dialed the numbers, "Meet me
at 1800...you know where." *Click. Once again he is feeling very*
good about himself.

As he started formulating his plan of action one of his
grandmother's proverbs, she use to quote to his father and
grandfather, came to his mind. "Where there is strife, there is pride,
but wisdom is found in those who take advice." (Proverbs 13:10).
He smiled, "Grams, even in death you are the wisest member
of this family. I'm sure there is a lesson in here for me, but I
need to teach a few others a lesson. No one threatens me and

gets away clean...no one." *He laughs* "They forget I know where ALL the bodies are buried!"

But that still small voice said, "and so does EN1 Harvey".

Chapter 17

"Charlie's"

*C*harlie's is a little bar and grill, "almost" dive, a couple of blocks from the naval base, off Hampton Boulevard, Norfolk, VA. It's owned by an old Navy friend of Scotty's from his other life as an enlisted soldier while living in the tri-service barracks at Fort Myers Army Base in Arlington, Virginia.

The music is blues and jazz, and on Friday and Saturday nights they have live bands. The food is decent, perfect for coating the belly when you plan to do a lot of drinking. Charlie is a cool dude, but he will let anybody know he runs a "clean establishment" and he don't mind putting rowdy folks, drunk or sober, out of his place. They can go on their own peaceably, or with the use of his boot. Either is fine with him.

Scotty goes to Charlie's when he wants to return to his roots. It reminded him of some of the places he and his friends went when he was living at Fort Myers.

Scotty arrived a few minutes early to have a drink by himself, and to make sure his thoughts were in order. Tonight was about business, but he also wanted it to be a relaxing time, just winding down with some blues. He looked at his watch with a frown, 1758.

"Commander."

"I'm glad you could make it, late."

She frowned and looked at her watch, "You said 1800. It's 1759. I'm here, how can I help you?

"You can come over here and tell me how much you missed me all day."

Sonya laughed and sat down asking herself, "¡¿Qué quieres?!" *("What do you want?!")*

Scotty was a little surprised, "Okay, have a seat. What can I get you?"

"Unsweet iced tea with lemon, thank you."

"Really? That's all, you don't want anything to eat?"

"No, I'm not hungry. I might get something to go later."

As Scottie goes to the bar, he is wondering what is going on with her. Did Nattie say something to her about him, about them? Or maybe she knows Nattie is getting close to the truth.

123

When he returns with the drinks, he asks again, "You sure you don't want anything else?

"I'm sure. Why did you order me to meet you here?"

Scotty was a little taken back by her directness. She is usually happy to see him.

"Um, is something wrong? Did you have a bad day? I didn't order you…"

Sonja sat back in her chair with her arms crossed, "I assumed you momentarily lost your mind considering how you ordered me here and then hung up the phone." *There was no lovey-dovey smile in her voice.*

"Yes, it was a bad day."

"And you decided to take it out on me?"

Now Scotty realizes he made a mistake, "Um, no, no, no, it's been one craziness after another all day. And then on top of it all, the mess about Jackson and Harvey. It's really raking on my nerves. I didn't mean…"

Sonja interrupted him, "And you thought your bad day was more important than my day. You thought because you were having a bad day you could disrupt my day and it would be alright? ¿Quién te crees que eres? (Who do you think you are?) You can't talk to me any-kind-of-way!

He reached across the table for her hand, " I'm sorry, I wasn't thinking. I was mad. I'm sorry…please don't be angry." *While he's talking he's thinking he does not have time for this. She needs to stop talking so that he can tell her his plan. He also knows if he wasn't careful with his words and tone she would walk out.* "Come on, don't be mad…please."

Sonja just looks at him thinking about how beautiful his eyes were, especially when he was pretending to be sorry. Being angry with him was a waste of energy she could devote to something more productive.

"Scotty, why did you call me here? I know you very well and so I know you want something. What is it? And don't say you want me, because I know you don't."

He chuckled, "You don't pull no punches do you? For your information, ma'am, I do need you but that's not why I called you. I need to know what's going on with Dr. Morgan. Why is she still asking questions? Why is she so concerned about what happens to Jackson or Harvey? When I called her this morning she had the gall to hang-up on me! She hung up on…"

The entire time he is rattling on, Sonja is looking at him as if he had lost his mind. When the waiter came by she asked for a to-go cup. At that point Scottie stops talking.

"What?! Where are you going, we just got here?"

"This whole deal is your mess, not mine. I don't have to give you explanations about what goes on onboard my ship. You're the lawyer, why didn't you call the legal officer if you wanted an update. You can, however, tell me what you really want from me now. Because, I'm about tired of this hide-and-seek game you all are playing." *Again, no love in her voice or in the expression on her face.*

At that moment he forgot he needed her. "Sonja, don't act like you are not getting something out of this. You stand to gain..."

Sonja lowered her voice to subdue her agitation, "What exactly am *I* getting out of it...revenge for being treated like a sub-human? I'm not the only one on that ship to benefit. He treats everyone like garbage, just like before. And besides, I still don't trust you after I told you who he was and you chose to hold the information about his past, after I told you how he treated me when I worked with him before. And every time I told you what was going on with him, you still chose to keep it to yourself. Now what, are you gonna tell me it's attorney – client privilege! Please, give me a break!"

Scotty tried to respond, but he could not get a word in, and the angrier she got, the thicker her accent became and she interchanged between Spanish and English, so it was good he was able to pay attention in English and Spanish.

Looking around to see if anyone is watching, "Look you need to calm down. Yes, I knew what he'd done and I wasn't looking for you to be in a position to expose him. But…"

Now she is furious and desperately trying to keep her voice down, not so much for Scotty, but she didn't want Charlie to make her leave before she got something to eat. "You Sir, are a snake from the pit of hell. You don't care who you use to get whatever it is you want. Sometimes, I hate you. And then sometimes, like now, I really hate you!" *Sonja sits back with her arms crossed. She is breathing hard and her heart is racing. Scotty could see he was not getting anywhere. So he does what he always does when women are mad at him, he pours on the honey. He moves his chair so he can touch her and speak softly, in Spanish and English, in her ear…*

"Por favor, mi amor, por favor no te enojes. Please, mi amor, please don't be mad. I'm sorry you really hate me right now, because I love you and I don't want you to be mad. I was gonna see if you were hungry yet. ¿Tienes hambre ahora? Are you hungry now? Should I order your regular?"

Still seething, "Is this your idea of love...ordering me around like I work for you...I don't work for you!

I'm sorry, I promise to do better. ¿Tienes hambre ahora?"

"Si, and don't forget the extra pickles! And seasoned curly fries not straight! Gracias! "

"Yes ma'am."

"Don't think just because I'm letting you feed me that I'm done with you!"

"I hope not!" *as he bent over to kiss her on his way to the bar to order their food.*

Scotty knew this mess had lingered on too long. It was time to either scrap it or bring it out into the open. If "he" had not threatened him, more than once, then it would not have come to this. He knows that if Dr. Morgan keeps digging, she will find exactly what she is looking for. And that would drag him down the sewer, and Sonja with him. He can't let that happen.

As he returned to the table, he looked at Sonja. He thought about all of the other failed relationships he's had, especially with Nattie. He thought about how most of the time he was the reason the relationships failed. He actually wanted this to work, but he knew he messed it up by dragging her into this mess. He has to figure out how to fix the mess and save his relationship with her.

"Your order will be ready shortly ma'am. *He pulled the chair closer to her.*

"You are right, I've been less than a gentleman about this whole mess. I'm sorry I dragged you into it. I never thought about using you in any way that would jeopardize your career or your reputation. And, I don't want this or anything to jeopardize us."

He leaned just close enough to kiss her, but he didn't. He waited. He wanted her to know he wasn't taking anything from her again. So he waited. Then, she leaned in and let him kiss her.

The waiter cleared his throat as he stood with the food.

"Oh! Thank you very much, this looks delicious," *Sonja replied as she blushed.*

Scotty looked at her with his serious eyes, "I have an idea that will close this case, without putting your or my career in jeopardy, but you really have to be onboard, and you have to get him onboard, otherwise it won't work."

So, he begin to tell her his plan. And, she listened.

Chapter 18

Thursday, September 23, 1999, 10 a.m.

Commander Janice Miller, Executive Officer

"Truth be told...or not?"

"*D*r. Morgan, please have a seat."

"Good morning Commander Miller, thank you for seeing me."

"Forgive me for not being able to see you earlier. We have been very busy getting ready for an upcoming exercise. Dr. Morgan I know you have been very busy trying to untie all of the knots concerning this case."

I thought to myself that was an interesting analogy..."untie all of the knots." I have today to finish this investigation and there are too many knots. Hmmm.

"Yes ma'am, and I'm hoping you will be able to help me solve this case so that we all can get back to our duties."

"Commander, can you give me your opinion of what you think this case is really all about?"

"As you know Dr. Morgan, the inquiry was filed by Petty Officer Jackson's mother who felt her son was being discriminated against because of his religion. I spoke to Petty Officer Harvey and Petty Officer Jackson and determined there was no case, which is why I originally dismissed it. I was surprised when we received word that you were still investigating it. Our lawyer assured us there was no further action needed and…"

"Excuse me ma'am, are you speaking of Lieutenant Wilson?" *I could tell by the astonished look on her face she wasn't expecting me to ask that question. Humm, again.*

"Um no Dr. Morgan. Lieutenant Wilson is our legal officer, not the investigating lawyer."

"He is a lawyer, yes?" *Again, that look.*

"Yes, just not for this case." I am referring to Commander Scott.

"Ah yes, the attorney who came to my office without an appointment and out of order. He told you the case was cleared. I'm not sure why he would have told you that. The case is far from being cleared. Commander, as I'm sure you recall, the inquiry also included an accusation of discrimination stating Petty Officer Jackson was being deliberately prevented from submitting an officer package. I..."

"Dr. Morgan, neither I nor Captain Grayson know of any effort to suppress Petty Officer Jackson's ability to submit a package."

"Commander Miller, it is my understanding the package has already been submitted."

She shifted her weight in her seat just a little, maybe hoping I didn't notice. She stated in a slightly agitated voice, "What exactly are you insinuating Dr. Morgan."

"Commander, my assignment from Congresswoman Abraham is to investigate this case and provide recommendations to resolve it. It is not my intent to be rude nor disrespectful. At the same time, I expect the same courtesy and cooperation directed towards me."

"Dr. Morgan everyone on this ship was instructed to give you whatever information you needed to resolve this situation." *Her body language clearly tells me that is not the entire truth and her goal is to get rid of me as soon as possible.*

"Thank you. Did you approve Petty Officer Jackson's request and package?"

"The Captain and I both approved his request, but I have not seen his completed package. Has NCC Franklin not been able to provide you all of the answers you need. She is the one that should be aware of the status of his request."

"We are working with an unofficial copy of the package, minus the signatures of you and the commanding officer. The original package is now missing."

"What do you mean missing?"

Now it is my turn to have a bewildered and frustrated look on my face. Especially since I know Chief Franklin spoke to her about the package being missing.

"I was told the original package disappeared over the weekend. Chief Franklin has turned over almost every rock on this ship trying to find it. If we only look at the signatures, the last person to see the original package is the Admin Officer. She doesn't know what happened to it. No one seems to know what happened to it. So, I'm asking again, what is really going on?

Obviously avoiding my questions, "Again, Dr. Morgan, what exactly are you insinuating? What exactly do you need from me to conclude your investigation? I'm sure you have more interesting cases awaiting you in Atlanta. As I said, our lawyer assured us that this inquiry was settled."

"Well ma'am, I will be talking to Commander Scott. Maybe he has information I don't have that will answer more of the questions? In the meantime, Commander Miller, contrary to what he may have told you, this case is far from being resolved."

"Dr. Morgan, if the package is missing then I suppose if Jackson really wants the appointment, he will submit another package. How hard can that be?"

I had to smile because it's been a while since I saw such an obvious display of not-my-problem. That makes me wonder what it is she is not telling me.

"Commander, you said the lawyer assured you this inquiry was settled. Where and when was it settled? And, if it was settled, why am I here?"

The commander sat silent for at least 45 seconds. I could tell she was trying not to make another mistake with her words.

So I stood and headed for the door. "Commander, today is the last day of investigations on the ship. Tomorrow morning I will take my findings back to Atlanta and in a couple weeks Captain Grayson, and the Fleet Commander will receive my recommendations. In one week, the program Petty Officer Jackson is applying for will be closed. This inquiry is about discrimination. I'm just not sure if it is racial or if it is status related. Also, I have already concluded that Petty Officer Harvey is somehow involuntarily involved in this chaos. If that is so then, Commander Miller, you have two harassment / discrimination cases on your hands. So, I would appreciate assistance, not resistance, from you in resolving this case."

"Dr. Morgan, as I said, I have not received the package for signature, therefore, he has one week to get me a new package. If he loses his opportunity, it will be on him, not me, or Captain Grayson."

It is taking every ounce of my strength to maintain my anger right now so that I can provide the respect her position dictates..

"Commander, someone is telling lies and instigating hate and discontent on your ship. I have been here three days and

I can see it. Someone is playing a deadly game of chess, using Petty Officers Jackson and Harvey as pawns. I will get to the bottom of it, with or without your assistance. I have already taken up too much of your time and mine. Good day."

"Dr. Morgan I'm sure we will talk again before you leave tomorrow. If anyone continues to be uncooperative, please let me know."

"Thank you."

As I stepped into the passageway from her office a saying of my dad's came to my mind. "Sometimes a liar cain't discern between a whole lie, and a partial truth." Well, I'm headed to the club and I'm not gonna ruin my night trying to figure out how many lies and partial truths I've been told while on this ship.

And after the club, I get to talk to Tracy. I really need to reach over and touch him, but I'll settle for hearing his voice tonight. We have so little time left. I hate I'm wasting part of it here, in this madness. But, Praise God, joy will be coming in the morning when I turn this rental car into Norfolk International Airport...Atlanta bound.

Chapter 19

Friday, September 24, 1999 – 7:35 a.m.

"What a wake-up call"

RING! RING! RING!

*N*attie could hear her cellphone ringing, but she couldn't remember where it was. She's surprised it still works because the last thing she remembered was hanging up on Tracy and throwing the phone across the room!

RING! RING! RING!

Nattie crawls out of bed and follows the noise. When she finally finds it whoever called had left a voice mail for her.

"Dr. Morgan, if you want to know the truth about the GREENWOOD LAKE, there will be a package waiting for you on the Quarterdeck when you arrive to the ship. Inside you will find everything you need to know."

I listened to the message several times trying to see if I'd heard the voice before. I had not. That ship is getting more mysterious by the minute.

RING! RING! RING!

"Good morning, this is Doctor..."

"Nattie, where are you?! This is Pat! Where are you?! Are you on your way?"

"I'm still at the hotel. What is wrong? I just got the weirdest phone call."

"How fast can you get to the ship! You have got to get here now! NOW!"

"Pat, what is going on! I have to..."

"I gotta go...COME NOW!"

Lord, what has happened. First this cryptic voice mail and then Pat hysterical. What is going on! Oh God, please don't let someone be hurt or something terrible has happened.

"Request permission to come aboard."

"Permission granted. Good morning Dr. Morgan. There is a package here for you. We were instructed to make sure you received it personally."

"Who instructed you?"

"The last watch. They said it was left with a note. The note is there. They don't know who left it or how it got left without them seeing the person that brought it. I understand you are leaving today. I'm sure you are ready to leave this zoo. It's been a pleasure meeting you."

"Yes and thank you. I have had an interesting four days. I can say it brought back many old zoo memories. You have a great day yourself."

Just as she was headed to the Chief's Mess, she saw Senior Chief Anthony.

"Patricia what is going on! Someone left me this package."

"I know, someone left one for Beth and Master Chief Hudson. It is not good. Not good at all. They are all here waiting for you."

"Who is 'they' and why are they waiting for me?"

"You'll see."

As I walked in, Master Chief Hudson, Beth, and Lieutenant Wilson were sitting there. Now I know something is really wrong that Lieutenant Wilson is in the Chief's Mess.

Master Chief Hudson started just as a cup of Earl Grey tea was placed in front of me.

"Dr. Morgan I know you are wondering what is going on here and why Lieutenant Wilson is..."

"Please call me Zach. Please."

"Zach is here."

"I see you received an envelope. So did Zach, Beth and I. It has instructions."

"Instructions?" *That's when I realized I had not looked at my envelope once it was handed to me.* "Don't open until you are all together."

"What? Jonathan what does yours say? Lieutenant Wilson, um, Zach, do you have any idea what is going on?"

"Only one part. The rest is a mystery to me as well. I'm sure you've been told I'm just here to "go-for" whatever anyone else won't. I'm normally only told what is absolutely required, and no more", *he sighed. The anguished look on his face told the story of his life since reporting to this ship.*

Jonathan continues, "We were all given this package when we arrived onboard this morning. I did not know who the "all" was, not until Zach came to my office to ask permission to meet with all of us in the Chief's Mess. His note also included the names of everyone required to be here and who would have envelopes."

Zach continues, "As you can see the envelopes are numbered in sequence and should be opened in that order. Master Chief, is it okay if I call you Jonathan…"

"Yes, first names are okay in here only."

"Thank you. Jonathan your envelope is first."

There was complete silence as Johnathan opened his envelope and poured out the contents. In it was a letter.

"Master Chief Hudson and Senior Chief Anthony. I thank you for always trying to help me do the right thing. I know that sometimes I get a little crazy and go off the deep end. I've been talking to someone about my anger and some of the crazy things I do. I've never had anyone act like they cared about me, not my family, not even my ex-wife. She just wants the money. She knows if I retire she will get a big check…well, she thinks it will be big and I'm not telling her any different. Chief Anthony, my girls say they love me and I guess that something, right? There's a picture of my girls. You can have it if you want. Anyway, I don't have anything against Jackson, except that he's smarter than anyone I know and

just as annoying. Yes, I'm jealous of people like him because they always seem to point out the slackers without even knowing it. I could have been a great engineman if I had not listened to my father. But I'm about to be an old man and I can't continue to blame him. I know I'm never going to make Chief and I'm good with that. I'm just trying to survive until I can retire. I know Jackson will make a good officer, but I just don't want to have to work for him. That would be cause for a suicide watch. Anyway, I know I have a disciplinary board coming up and I'm not asking for any favors. I know people have been telling Dr. Morgan that I stole his package, but I just wanted you to know I don't have Jackson's package. They blamed me on my last ship, so I'm not surprised they blame me here".

Pat: "Wow! Wow! Never in a million years would I have seen that coming, except you remember I said there's more going on with him than what we see. Like seeing a therapist. I never knew."

Nattie: "What does he mean they blamed him on his last ship and they are blaming him now. What is he talking about?

Jonathan handed Pat the picture, and continued reading, "There needs to be an investigation about everything he has done. When that happens, I'm willing to say what really happened on my last ship and on this one. Like I said, I'm not looking for any favors. People like him and my dad should be punished because of the way they treat people smaller than they are. My dad is dead in hell, so there's nothing to be done about him. But…well, just let me know if you need me. If I'm going to prison, I'd like it to be for a worthy cause. "

Jonathan placed the letter back in the envelope.

Zach: Doc, you have the second envelope.

Nattie hesitated before she opened her envelope. Lord, Lord… When she emptied her envelope there were letters, copies of request chits, and what look like official court documents.

"Dr. Morgan, I'm sure you have a very bad taste in your mouth for me. I hurt you so long ago and now that you have definitely surpassed me in greatness, I wasn't sure how to handle it. I have NEVER had anyone talk to me the way you did and still do. After I stopped fuming, I realized you were correct. Nattie, contrary to what you may believe, I did not know you were Dr. Natalee Morgan. I just assumed there were other women who spelled their name the way you did. So, no, I did not come to Atlanta with a preconceived scheme in mine. When I was in your office I saw a file that told me you will keep digging until you release all of the skeletons, so, I'm gonna help you. Enclosed in this envelope is everything you need to

identify the real problems and who is the instigator of these problems. I'm sure you will know what to do and it still be within the realms of your investigation. Keep doing what you do. The world needs more people like you defending the underdog."

Nattie looked at Zach and then at the papers in front of her, "Why did he send me this. I already know some of this, but I didn't tell him that. I'm still confused as to how it all fits."

Zach: "I cannot tell you anything you don't already know. However, I will be your Boy-Friday and do whatever legwork you need done up here. And, you need to tell them what the papers are."

Nattie, looking around the table at each of them. Then she passed papers around to each of them. For a moment, all could be heard was gasps and "Oh my God, what the...".

Nattie explained, "When I first received this case, my assistant and I did a quick background check on both Petty Officers Harvey and Jackson, as well as, Captain Grayson so that we could get an idea of what we might be up against. I remembered your Captain Grayson's name, but I could not remember why. Nancy, my assistant, found an old article about an incident that happened in New Orleans several years ago involving a harassment / discrimination case filed by several females that should have been investigated, but was dismissed at the command level. I've been trying to discern what has that to do with this."

Zach chimed in, "I think my package will answer that question. I have the packet number three."

Zach opened his envelope. Inside were more legal papers, which he passed around to each of them. The letter inside read...

"This case came to my desk because a crewmember onboard the ship filed a complaint against her commanding officer. Such complaints are taken very seriously, however, the information we received from her and the information we received from the ship were in conflict with each other. We did our due diligence and determined the case did not have enough information to warrant further actions, and so the command's initial verdict stood. However, there was enough evidence to warrant transferring the sailor to another ship, which we recommended to the proper people. Because there was a previous incident concerning this commanding officer, the Judge Advocate determined that it would be in the best interest of the Navy to transfer the commanding officer without the possibility of further promotion and in preparation for early retirement, as well as, without any further disciplinary action, which also happened. You and Dr Morgan will have to put the two previous incidents together, to discover what really happened and how it manifested itself

onboard the GREENWOOD LAKE. Also, in the last incident, there were two enlisted people jeopardized. The female was transferred. The male was not. He was the scapegoat. The sailor is EN1 Harvey. Yes, he did harass the women, but there was more to the story. He is again, the scapegoat and there is still more to the story. At his last command, even though the case was dismissed, he was treated as the guilty party. When the ship changed homeports, they were able to transfer him to the GREENWOOD LAKE…to be someone else's problem. Your executive officer, Commander Miller, does not have a clue about any of this; and it should stay that way. When Dr. Morgan and Zach complete their investigation, she will benefit, from plausible deniability. Besides, she has her own skeletons to tend with. If you and Zach need my assistance, which I expect you won't, I am at your disposal."

At this point, everyone around the table's eyes are glazed over. Master Chief signaled for another round of coffee.

Zack: "Beth you have the last envelope. Please open it."

Beth's hands were trembling while she tried to imagine what might be in her envelope. Inside her envelope was Jackson's complete, original package, signed by Commander Miller and Captain Grayson.

Beth: "I don't understand. Nattie didn't you tell me Commander Miller said she had not seen the package?" *Nattie nodded her head.* "I don't understand." *Then she noticed the letter attached to the package.*

Beth's voice is shaky as she begins, "Chief Franklin, please forgive me for withholding this information from you. It was the only leverage we had to fuel the feud between Harvey and Jackson so that we could send an anonymous note to Petty Officer Jackson's mother alerting her to the possibility of her son being discriminated against. I am very familiar with the policies of Jackson's faith when it comes to religious liberty, so I knew she would contact someone that could help her. I know my mother would turn over mountains if she knew the hardships I've endured, at two different commands. I had heard about the original incident long before I came to the GREENWOOD LAKE, but I didn't know details and I didn't worry about it, especially after he left. I assumed I would never see him again. Everyone on the ship knows he treated me horribly, because I'm a woman and because I'm Hispanic. I believe he had no intention of approving Jackson's request, but he had no valid reason not to, so he signed it. I have instructed PN1Richards to help you in any way she can to get Jackson's package to Federal Express today. We have already made three copies to be distributed as you see fit.

We will not say anything to Petty Officer Jackson. I thought you would like to tell him yourself. And to be clear, PN1 Richards was not involved. Actually, she would have blown the entire operation trying to protect Harvey. Dr. Morgan, I know you are angry with Scottie, but he helped me to put all of this together so justice will be served on all ends. It is, however, still up to you to continue the investigation if you choose. Just in case you need it, I mailed a congressional complaint to Congresswoman Abraham yesterday. In the letter I said I know I am not from Georgia. I am from Texas. I know I won't get any viable support from the congressman there, so I'm reaching out to her. I also asked her if you would be the investigator. I hope you don't mind. Although we did not have time to get acquainted, I hope you will allow me to keep in touch."

Everyone sat in complete silence for what seemed like forever.

Zach: "So, I'm sure your heads are still reeling. Beth I want to apologize for the part I played in this fiasco; however, I honestly had no clue what happened to the package. I know it's been a grueling few days. Dr. Morgan, I'm at your disposal. I've always wanted to come to Atlanta.

Pat: Petty Officer Harvey is not onboard right now, but I will talk to him when he comes to work.

Beth: "Let me find Jackson and let him know his package will be on a FEDEX truck this morning! Nattie, are you sure you have to leave today? Tonight is Margarita Nite at the Club.

Nattie: "I'd love too, but I have to go home. I had forgot how cold it is up here!

Everyone laughed saying it's not cold...yet.

Nattie laughed, "Even when it's cold in Atlanta, it's not this cold. I have to go home because I have a Lieutenant to reprimand. I'll be back, in a few months, when it's warmer, and you all can do Margarita Nite and I will be your designated driver. Or you all can always come to Atlanta. We have some nice hotels, restaurants and bars. You'll love it!"

"Zach," *Nattie hesitated,* "Who put all of these packages together? Whose idea was this?"

Zach smiled, "I'm sorry Nattie. Attorney-Client confidentiality?"

Everyone shook their heads as they headed in their separate directions.

Zach turning to Jonathan, "Thank you Master Chief for inviting me into the Chief's Mess. From what I've heard in the past, no one from the wardroom has ever been invited. I'm honored."

Jonathan smiled, "You are welcome."

Chapter 20

Epilogue

Friday, September 24, 1999

*D*ear Diary. I was a little sad saying my goodbyes as I walked off of the USS GREENWOOD LAKE. I am still a little bit overwhelmed about the events of this morning. Although the case is not closed, yet, I feel a sense of relief flow over me with the "appearance" of Jackson's original package, the friends I made and the unspoken "not completely closed-closure" between Scotty and me. I wonder, even though have I moved on, was a part of him still lingering, haunting my spirit all of these years. I wonder if that unconscious spirit was the reason I let go at the first hint of oppression in my relationships...in my marriage. I wonder? Well, even psychologist have demons lurking about. And besides, he has a girlfriend...that's too funny!"

I am finally at the airport to catch my plane to Atlanta. I'm here early because I hate running through the airport trying to make it to the gate before the flight attendant puts that chain across the entrance. *Who would imagine a chain so small would cause immediate anxiety. That almost happened to me once. Never again.*

I'm upset with Tracy. I've been retired for four years and I still love the Navy, but sometimes, like today, I really hate the Navy. He called me at 4:00 A.M. to tell me he would not be at the airport to pick me up and he would not be available until "sometime" on Sunday! Why?! His wife, Mrs. Navy, made plans for him without asking me if it was alright! I survived this entire week of crazy because I knew at the end of it he would be at the airport scooping me up in those massive arms, telling me how much he missed me. SHE RUINED IT! Right now, I really HATE her! UGH!

Since there is time, I want to look at some of my notes and copies of the letters from this morning, but my spirit is begging for a break. However, the clues to this case seem obvious, but there are still secrets hidden behind these words. The skeletons are screaming to be free and I have the key to all of the closets…on the lines of this mess of papers lying in my briefcase.

There are so many questions floating around in my head. Such as why, all of a sudden did Scotty shift colors? What does he stand to gain? In the last ten day since he walked into my office, I have been able to see that, after 20 plus years, he has not changed. Actually, he has grown into more of a narcissist. This made it easier to see that I made the right choice not to run after him that night.

Or, is that what I wanted to see to make it easy to stay detached from him? Hmmm.

What is the relationship between the three letter writers? They have nothing in common...or do they? What is up with Commander Scott and Lieutenant Alejandro! She clearly called him "Scotty" in her letter. I'm smiling because I know there is a story there. I hope it's one that will settle him down. That would be a miracle.

Well, I know Nancy, along with her new intern Lieutenant Zach Wilson, will get to the bottom of this barrel. I suspect that Lieutenant Wilson knows more of the names, dates and places then he has let on. Will he, I wonder, continue to keep them in his closet, and what will entice him to open the door?

Well, I'm not going to worry about any of this this weekend, Monday will be here soon enough.

Right now, I need to find some tea. I'm sure one of these eating establishments serves Earl Grey, hot, with cream and honey...and maybe a hint of...

Chapter 21

Some Facts About

Borderline Personality Disorder and

Narcissist Personality Disorder

(This narrative is for informational purposes only. Consult your physician or licensed mental health provider for diagnosis and treatment)

<u>Borderline Personality Disorder</u>

*B*orderline Personality Disorder (BPD) is a mental disorder characterized by an instability in mood, behavior, and functioning. It impacts the way a person thinks and feels about him or herself and others. This can cause problems functioning in everyday life and interacting with others. BPD can include issues with self-image, difficulty managing emotions, behavior and anger, along with a pattern of dysfunction in regard to relationships. Many times BPD cause people to create unwarranted problems or "drama" within their environment. Also evident are impulsive and risky behavior, such as gambling, reckless driving, unsafe sex, spending sprees, binge eating or drug abuse, or sabotaging success by suddenly quitting a good job or ending a positive relationship.

BPD is more common than one would think. In the United States alone there are more than three million documented cases per year. It usually begins by early adulthood and seems to worsen during young adulthood. Fortunately, episodes seem to dissipate gradually as they age. A diagnosis of BPD is not made in children or teenagers, because what appear to be signs and symptoms of BPD may go away as children get older and become more mature.

BPD is commonly treated with much success using psychotherapy, also called talk therapy. Your therapist may adapt the type of therapy to best meet your needs. The goals of psychotherapy are to help you:

- Focus on your current ability to function

- Learn to manage emotions that feel uncomfortable

- Reduce your impulsiveness by helping you observe feelings rather than acting on them

- Work on improving relationships by being aware of your feelings and those of others

- Learn about borderline personality disorder

Currently medication for BPD has not been approved by the Food and Drug Administration. However, certain medications may help with symptoms or co-occurring issues such as depression, impulsiveness, aggression or anxiety.

Narcissistic Personality Disorder

Narcissistic Personality Disorder (NPD) is a mental disorder with exaggerated feelings of self-importance, but low self-esteem. NPD a type of personality disorders normally identified when people have an inflated sense of their own importance, a deep need for excessive attention and admiration, troubled relationships, and a lack of empathy for others. But behind this mask of extreme confidence lies a fragile self-esteem that's vulnerable to the slightest criticism. NPD causes problems in many areas of life, such as relationships, work, school or financial affairs. People tend to be generally unhappy and disappointed when they're not given the special favors or admiration they believe they deserve. They may find their relationships unfulfilling, and others may not enjoy being around them.

NPD is another very common disorder with more than 3 million documented cases per year in the United States alone. NPD is treatable by a mental health professional, preferably a psychiatrist or psychotherapist. It is normally detected between the ages 18-35 and is commonly found in males.

NPD is best treated using talk therapy or psychotherapy which helps to...

- Learn to relate better with others so your relationships are more intimate, enjoyable and rewarding.

- Understand the causes of your emotions and what drives you to compete, to distrust others, and perhaps to despise yourself and others.

- Currently medication may be subscribed for symptoms or co-occurring issues such as depression, impulsiveness, aggression or anxiety.

If you, or someone you know, displays any of these behaviors talk to your doctor or a mental health provider.

Reliable information pertaining to these mental health disorders can be found on the Mayo Clinic Website.

Borderline personality disorder - Symptoms and causes - Mayo Clinic

Narcissistic personality disorder - Diagnosis and treatment - Mayo Clinic

Thank you for being a fan of Earl Grey Chronicles. Book 3, A State of Affairs: Revelation will be launched Summer, 2023. To make sure you don't miss it, please allow me to email you about my books, book reading and signing events, as well as my services as a Christian Life Coach. Join my email listing at NeverSayCain't Christian Life Coach and Consultant

https://transitionlifecoach4u.com/contact

> *"Behold, I will bring it health and healing; I will heal them and reveal to them **the abundance of peace and truth.**"*
> *~Jeremiah 33:6 (NKJV)*